PLAY

C.S. BARNES

ALSO BY C.S. BARNES

Intention

Copycat

1

M r Noland was talking to the class about the importance of citing their research. But the back row wasn't listening. The seats were occupied by the so-called popular boys who, one nudge at a time, were passing a phone among themselves while their teacher went on with his lesson. The handset that the students were sharing soon reached the end of the row, at which point Benjamin Castle – or Benji to his friends – leaned forward and tapped another boy on the shoulder.

'Don't give it to him,' Aiden Harris whispered from two seats away.

'Is there a problem at the back?' Mr Noland weighed in.

'No, sir, no problem,' Benji replied.

Aiden's intervention had come too late: the iPhone had already changed hands and another boy was watching the same video that the back row club had been privy to. The boy passed the phone to a girl who passed the phone to someone else. A small emotional explosive, it moved around the room at four-minute intervals, changing hands whenever one viewer became bored with the content.

'They're not even getting to the best bit,' Aiden whispered

again. The comment was made more to himself but Rhys Wilkins – another student who had watched the video in its entirety – gave a grumble of agreement. 'It's bloody wasted in here,' Aiden said, speaking along the row to Benji.

'Harris, what's the problem?' Mr Noland asked.

The boy sat upright. 'Nothing, sir. There isn't a problem.'

'Then maybe your discussion could wait until you're outside of my classroom?'

Mr Noland was one of the more laid-back teachers in the school. Even when he reprimanded the students, he didn't really reprimand them. When Harris gave his tutor a nod of agreement, and a swift apology – 'Sorry again, sir.' – Mr Noland turned back to writing examples of good referencing on the board.

The iPhone changed hands one final time before the lesson finished. Damien Fuller, the quiet boy who remained an outcast, despite his best efforts to bond with his classmates, took the phone from the girl sitting next to him and hit play. He wasn't even sure what he was being given, but in a bid to fit in Damien always went along with these things. The others watched from the back of the room, their eyes widening, their hands fidgeting with whatever was in front of them, as they one by one realised that unlike everyone else, Damien was going to watch the whole thing.

'Shit.'

'Shit, indeed.'

The boys talked in whispers as Damien watched on, apparently neutral to the content. Benji glanced at his watch and saw that it had been a good five minutes now, and he had to admit, he was impressed that Fuller had lasted this long; Benji wouldn't have thought the other boy had it in him. *The video must be close to finishing by now*, he thought, there could only be a few seconds–

'Oh my God.' The small eruption came from Damien who, hand over mouth, looked up to see the class's attention shifting focus from the whiteboard and settling on him. The boy, small in stature, sank back in his chair and stared up at his teacher who was standing in front of his desk.

'Is that something you want to show me, Fuller?' Mr Noland asked, eyeing the phone.

Damien nodded. 'Yes, sir, I think it is.'

There was a collective gasp in the room. Mr Noland looked as though he might have contributed towards it. In his years of teaching there hadn't been a time when a student had handed over a phone so readily; although there hadn't been a student in his class who had turned so ghostly pale either. Mr Noland reached forward to lift the phone and in doing so caught sight of the video preview. He gave Damien a quick nod.

'Shall we step outside for this?' the teacher asked, and again Damien agreed. Mr Noland turned to address the class. 'Look through the research you've done for your coursework. By the time I come back in, I want at least half of those references to be written out in full using these patterns,' he said, gesturing to the board. 'Shall we?' he said, facing Damien, and the two marched from the classroom, the door falling shut behind their exit.

'Fuck's sake, we never should have let it get that far around the class,' Benji blurted out, thumping the desk as he spoke. 'Fuller was obviously going to shit himself over it.'

Ceri Mason, who was sitting in front of the boys, turned around abruptly to face her classmate. 'You never should have brought porn into class, full stop. What are you, a bunch of bloody animals?'

The boys swapped amused looks among themselves.

'You didn't even watch it, did you?' Wilkins said. 'Like we'd bring porn into school with us. We're not as stupid as you think, you know.'

'Yeah, we're not as stupid as you th–'

'Harris, Castle, Wilkins.' The sound of their surnames cut across the general murmurings of the room, forcing the class into an uncomfortable quiet. Mr Noland stood in the open doorway with Fuller just visible behind him. 'The three of you can stay where you are for the time being, everyone else is dismissed.' He stepped into the room to clear the doorway for the fleeing students. 'As always, thank you for your participation. I'll see you all later in the week.' The teacher was polite to his students; he'd always thought that treating them like adults would trick them into acting like adults, although the theory had been proved wrong today. Mr Noland gestured Damien back into the room before approaching the fearful-looking boys that were left at the back of the class. The teacher's top show may have been calm and collected, but as he approached the offenders, with the iPhone gripped inside a whitened fist, Mr Noland couldn't help thinking: *A murder, and in my classroom.*

2

DI Melanie Watton set the phone on her desk and leaned back in her chair. Since the copycat case that they dealt with last year, everything around the office had been comfortably quiet. DS Edd Carter and DC Chris Burton had been taking burglary cases while DCs Brian Fairer and David Read had been taking as little as possible, and they thought their boss hadn't noticed. Meanwhile, DC Lucy Morris spent most of her days with her head in or under a computer, with the technology team teaching her enough to make her the resident tech person in Melanie's office.

The mundane cases had been a welcome arrival, and she couldn't blame her team for needing a break from the big reveals. She checked the time before pushing herself away from the desk and heading to her open doorway. Melanie propped herself against the frame before calling out to Burton. 'Have you submitted paperwork on that break-in?'

Burton hit the enter button on her keyboard with a deliberate emphasis. 'Just.' She turned to smile at her superior. 'Not bad for a morning's work, eh?'

'You're not missing the thrill of hunting a killer yet?' Melanie asked, her tone one of sarcasm. The two officers had discussed this already and they'd both decided that their killer-days were ones they could happily not return to. The case had put Melanie on the map in terms of her leadership and investigative skills – but she wasn't sure it was a map she wanted to be marked on. The only member of her team who seemed hungry for that same level of intensity again was–

'Morning all,' Carter said as he opened the office door with a swift kick. 'I brought doughnuts because it's Friday.'

'It's Thursday,' Burton corrected him without missing a beat.

Carter looked from his partner to Mel, who gave a quick nod to confirm the announcement. He shrugged.

'Well, arses. I brought doughnuts because it's Thursday.' He amended his remark but used the same enthusiasm. He set the tray of doughnuts on the centre table and before he'd managed to get to his own desk, Fairer and Read had already flocked to the baked goods. 'Do you two not get fed at home?'

'We don't get fed doughnuts at home,' Fairer replied, his mouth already full. Read, his cheeks bulging with what Carter guessed was an entire doughnut, nodded in agreement with his partner.

'Any occasion for doughnuts?' Mel asked.

'It's nearly the weekend and I'm in a good mood, that's all,' Carter said, facing his computer monitor as he waited for his login details to register. Behind him, Melanie and Burton shared a knowing look. It was nearly Carter's weekend with his daughter, Emily, and Melanie could set his mood changes by these custody arrangements. Carter and his wife, Trish, had only separated six months ago after a drawn-out attempt at making their marriage work. There had been a noticeable lift in the man's mood since the divorce proceedings started, and his co-workers were relieved to see a spring back in his step – and doughnuts on the table.

The computer finally kicked into life and Carter checked his emails. 'Have we got anything fresh in today, Chris?'

'Nothing that I'm aware of. I've signed off on the Chamberton Street case, so we're finalising paperwork for everything else today,' Burton said, turning to face her own screen. Carter let out a dramatic sigh but the DC held a steady look at her computer. 'What now?'

'Don't you want something more interesting, Burton?'

'Have you acquired a death wish, DS Carter?' Melanie weighed in before her DC could answer. 'We managed to solve cases just fine before Eleanor Gregory dragged us into her affairs, and we'll manage the average-Joe break-ins and arson attacks just fine now.' The DI spoke in a jovial tone but there was something serious in her sentiment.

Carter put both hands palm up in a symbol of submission. 'I don't have anything against arsonists,' he said, matching her tone.

Melanie opened her mouth to reply but the sound of her desk phone ringing pulled her back into her office.

'C'mon, Burton, you're telling me you aren't a touch bored?' Carter pushed.

Burton turned around to face him. 'Yes, alright, I am a touch bored.' Carter threw his head back in a display of delight. 'But,' Burton said pointedly to catch his attention again, 'I don't mind being bored for a while, Edd.'

The two worked in silence for a minute longer until the DI came to stand in her open doorway again. Her eyebrows were angled into a frown as she studied a small square Post-it note. A few seconds rolled by before Carter caught sight of his superior.

'What's got you stumped?' he asked.

'Report from a local school.' Melanie's stomach clenched at the sound of her own announcement; the last report from a local college had been enough. 'There's a video going around that the head teacher is concerned about and we've been asked to take a look at it.'

'Oh, well that just sounds like a really juicy–' Carter's tone was overblown with sarcasm, but Melanie cut across him as she stuck the Post-it note to his desk.

'Murder, it's a video of a murder?'

Burton stood up and grabbed her jacket from the back of her chair. 'You had to go and ask for something bloody interesting.'

3

Carter and Burton climbed into their shared vehicle and left the station, heading for the school. Melanie had given them all the information she had: a Dr Oakley, head teacher of Milton High School, had called to report a video that had been passed around the students, allegedly showing a murder. The head teacher hadn't expressed any thoughts on whether the video was real, only that the content was concerning. 'She might have used the word convincing,' Melanie added, before sending her officers on their way. It wasn't the first time a video like this had done the rounds, although they typically ended up being a make-up and staging nerd having a field day. It didn't hurt to verify matters though.

Carter rounded the corner of the final street and the car came face to face with a stretch of concrete that served as a playground, with a tall and imposing building positioned at the end of it. This looked like the sort of school he remembered going to, a hundred or so years ago. Without thinking, he expelled a heavy sigh.

'What now?' Burton asked, glancing at her colleague.

'What?'

'You sighed.'

Carter hesitated before answering. 'Doesn't it make you feel old, Chris, coming to places like this?' Burton was a good five years younger than Carter was, and they both knew it. But the information went unsaid until, 'I know I've got years on you but–'

'Carter, get it together. You've got a life in front of you and these kids have got detention and acne. Keep some perspective, eh?' she said, nudging his elbow and giving him a wink as he pulled into a visitor's space. 'Things aren't half as bad as you seem to think they are today.'

The two made their way into the building. After signing the necessary form they were escorted to the head teacher's office by a determined receptionist, who was adamant they wouldn't navigate the halls alone. *Whatever else is going on in the school*, Carter thought, *they're at least careful about letting anyone in – the police included, it seems.*

'What do you think this bloke will be like then? Strong and stern, or kind and approachable?' Carter asked as the receptionist rapped her knuckles against a closed office door.

From the other side someone granted them admission and as the older woman pushed the door open, she stepped to one side to allow the officers entry. Carter stepped into Dr Oakley's office to find a petite woman, no older than thirty-five, sitting behind a large and imposing desk. Burton walked by her colleague and gave him a deliberate knock as she passed him; Carter could see the smirk from her profile.

'Dr Oakley, I'm DC Chris Burton and this is my colleague DS Edd Carter,' she said, extending a hand to the head teacher who stood to greet them.

'A pleasure,' the woman replied, taking Burton's hand and giving it a firm shake. When the introductions were made the officers took their seats opposite the doctor and readied themselves for the early details.

Burton had a pen poised over her notepad when she asked, 'So, you called us here about a video?'

'Yes, a recording on an iPhone, although I'm told there are several phones around the school that have this content on them by now.' The irritation was clear in her tone. She had a kind face but Carter sensed the head teacher ran a tight ship. 'I won't beat around the bush, detectives, the clip shows a woman murdering someone. I've watched the whole thing myself and it's fairly unsavoury, as you can imagine.'

Burton scribbled away, giving Carter a moment to pick up the baton. 'Do you think it's real footage, Dr Oakley?'

The head teacher considered this with some concentration. When Burton looked up from her writing, the other woman finally answered. 'I honestly can't say. It's certainly convincing, but as for whether it's real or not, I'm not a doctor so I'm not qualified to comment.' Carter narrowed his eyes and Oakley laughed. 'I'm not that kind of doctor.'

'May we see the footage?' Burton asked.

'You can do better than see it; you can take the whole phone with you,' she said, reaching into a drawer. 'This handset belongs to a student called Benjamin Castle. I confiscated it, called his mother and made her aware I was involving the police. She's given me written confirmation via email that you're welcome to take this with you.' She nodded to the phone lying in the free desk space between her and the officers. 'I've made the students aware that anyone caught watching, distributing or even discussing the contents of the video will be suspended at least, banned from the school grounds at most.'

Carter was impressed.

'When did you discover the footage, Dr Oakley?' Burton continued.

'First period this morning. One of the teachers, a Mr Noland, found students watching it in his classroom.' She leaned forward and set a hand on her desk phone. 'I can call him in if you need to ask him any questions?'

'That won't be necessary,' Carter said.

'I was more curious about how quickly you'd acted on all of this,' Burton spoke again. 'You must be quite concerned about what's on this film.'

The head teacher shrugged. 'I know what teenagers are capable of, detective. Anything that puts stupid ideas in their heads isn't something that I welcome in my school.'

The detectives collected the phone and stashed it into an evidence bag for safekeeping. After thanking the head teacher for her time, they vacated the office and made their way back through the winding halls of the building. Carter was all too aware of the staring eyes and bobbing heads that appeared in windows and doorways to catch a glance at them leaving. He smiled on the walk out. Even now he could remember the excitement of police being called in to his school – never for anything quite so major as this though.

Burton signed them both out and followed Carter into the open playground.

'Well, that was swift,' Carter said, stepping down onto the concrete. 'She seems to know what she's about; that should make this whole thing easier to deal with.'

'Mm,' Burton agreed, her smile spreading. 'She was a nice bloke, wasn't she?'

4

Melanie sat at her desk with her DS and DC standing either side of her. In silence the three of them watched the video from start to finish. Carter moved to speak but paused as Melanie dragged the cursor back along the video's timer bar and re-started the footage at the point of the murder. Melanie shook her head and narrowed her eyes as it played out again. She and Burton sat through the footage for a second time, but Carter looked away from the screen. When the footage slowed to a blackout, Melanie right-clicked to exit the media player.

She rubbed at the back of her neck before gesturing to the chairs opposite her own. 'Come, sit, I want your thoughts.' Both officers came to sit in front of their boss. From their troubled expressions, Melanie could already see they were no more comfortable about this whole thing than she was. 'Is it real?'

There was a heavy beat of silence before Carter answered, 'It bloody looks real.'

'What do we know about this? Where did it come from, exactly?' Melanie asked.

'A kid in the school looks to have been passing it around his mates, and the head teacher said she has suspicions that it's been sent to other devices as well,' Burton replied. 'We have the kid's name. Can we speak to him.'

'Do you think we need to?' Carter chimed in.

Melanie narrowed her eyes again, as though physically inspecting something on her monitor. After two false starts of opening her mouth but having no words emerge, she eventually made a decision. 'I'm going to take this to the medical examiner's office.' She pushed back from her desk as she spoke. 'Waller might be more familiar with this sort of thing than we are, so he might have some thoughts to throw into the ring. Carter, can you get this onto one of our secured drives? I don't want the handset leaving the station.' Melanie tugged on her jacket before reaching for the phone. As she re-packaged it into an evidence bag, Burton broke the silence.

'Are we thinking this is real, boss?' There was a nervous edge to her voice.

Melanie let out a hard exhale. 'Put it this way, I'm not confident in assuming it isn't.'

Melanie and the local medical examiner, George Waller, hadn't seen a great deal of each other in the last twelve months since last year's copycat killing spree. They swapped the occasional email and half-promised the occasional coffee, but nothing had ever come of it. However, when Melanie stepped through the double doors into the open-plan office-cum-operating-suite, she felt as though no time had passed. She scouted around the space to eventually find George, wearing a pair of magnifying spectacles over his normal glasses, as he leaned down to stitch together the chest of a cadaver. Melanie couldn't hold in a heave which called up George's attention. He stared over the rim of his glasses to lock eyes with the detective, and a fire seemed to light beneath him. George snapped off his gloves in an uncomfortable gesture and dropped his glasses into a nearby evidence tray. In five great, deliberate strides he crossed the space and came to a halt three steps shy of Melanie, his arms folded. Melanie moved to speak – to apologise for whatever it was George clearly thought she'd done – but he held a hand up to halt her.

'Detective,' he started, 'you don't call, you don't write, and then after all these months–' On seeing Melanie's amused expression, George's introduction cracked into a harsh laugh. 'Who am I kidding? It's good to see you, Watton.' He gave her a light tap on the shoulder.

Melanie couldn't help but scrunch her face up at the kindness in this revised greeting. 'You might not think that in a second,' she replied, pulling the small evidence bag from her pocket. 'I have something I need your help with.'

Waller rolled his eyes. 'When don't you? You're allowed to meet people socially, you know, that's a thing too,' he said, padding back toward the body resting behind him. George pulled on a new pair of gloves and picked up the thread he'd been working with when Melanie arrived. 'What interesting and time-consuming thing have you brought for me?'

'It's something that you need to see for yourself, I think.'

George stood upright to face the DI. 'Mel, if it's police footage of my daughter being drunk and stupid then frankly, I have Facebook for that.'

Melanie couldn't help but crack a smile, despite the announcement she still had to make. 'We might have footage of someone being murdered,' she said, her voice tight.

The words caught George's attention. Once again he dropped his thread, snapped off his gloves, and closed in on Melanie.

'You've brought me a snuff film?' Where Melanie's voice had

sounded troubled, George's sounded more excited. 'An actual one, or a really good pretend one?'

'You tell me.' Melanie extended the portable drive that Carter had transferred the video to. 'Everything you need is on this and you should already have an email from Carter or Burton explaining how the drive works. Maybe when you've got a second–'

'Oh, I've got a second,' George cut across her, snatching the bag from her fingers. He crossed the office to the desk that was elevated on a small platform behind them both. George leaned forward to turn on his computer and said, 'I realise I have an inappropriate excitement, but you've brought me an urban myth, you realise?'

Melanie shrugged. 'I might have brought you exceptionally good special effects.'

'Either way, I'll need a little time to decipher this,' he said, taking a seat. 'Are you okay to wait or should I call through later?'

Melanie realised she didn't need to be here for this. She'd seen the whole video once, the murder twice, and that was enough for one early afternoon. She shook her head to decline the offer and back-stepped toward the door. 'I'm needed back at base for one or two things.'

'Suit yourself,' George replied, connecting the portable drive to a USB cable. 'I'll try to get an answer to you one way or another before the close of today.'

The DI wandered back through the halls and to the outside world. It wasn't until the fresh air hit her that she truly appreciated the clinical stench of the medical examiner's office. She'd spent far too much of her time there in her career to date, but she couldn't settle the suspicion that she'd have to spend more time there in the near future.

~

The open-plan office outside Melanie's own private one was nearly empty. Fairer and Read had left just over an hour ago, meanwhile DC Lucy Morris had gone straight home from her training with the technology team. Since the DC's show of aptitude for technology in last year's big case, she'd brushed elbows with different agencies around the country, and Melanie had to admit a flush of pride. Meanwhile, Carter and Burton were clearly locked in an anti-race, both of them trying not to leave their posts before their superior left hers. The officers eventually caved in unison, offering Melanie a 'See you tomorrow, boss,' and a 'Bye for now, then,' respectively. The DI was close to giving up on Waller's phone call but as she switched off her computer her desk phone kicked into life, and she was glad of the privacy she had to take the call.

'DI Watton,' she answered, on the off-chance it was someone else calling through. But it was, thankfully, George on the line.

'I'm sorry I've kept you waiting, Mel, I wanted to be sure before I called.' The jovial tone he'd taken earlier in the day had been replaced with something else. Melanie couldn't decide whether it was the type of tone that comes at the end of a long day, or one that accompanies bad news.

'What's the verdict, doc?'

'I've watched it as many times as I can stand to and I spoke to a colleague as well. I didn't show them anything, of course,' he added, before Melanie could interject. 'Look, without a body in front of me I can't give you any promises but from everything I've seen, Mel, this looks a lot like murder to me.'

5

After Melanie's phone call with Waller she went straight to his office to collect the offending portable drive. She wanted it logged into evidence before the close of the day. By the time she was arriving home, an hour later than expected, she was mentally drafting a message to her team. While the kettle boiled behind her, she pulled out her phone and typed:

Team meeting. I need everyone in for 7.30.

She spent the rest of the evening learning everything she could about these snuff films; including their myth-like status and the internet's fascination with them. There were one or two links she'd found useful, but she couldn't help but think she hadn't found the worst of it yet. Morris' first job in the morning was to check out the internet for more details than Melanie's potluck searching would find. She spent the hours after this planning everyone else's jobs. Fairer and Read would go back to the school, on the off-chance that there would be something useful hidden there. Morris would be best placed looking over the recording, Melanie eventually decided. That left Burton and Carter traipsing through the internet – if Morris could set them up with somewhere to start. All of this left Melanie with one crucial but uncomfortable job to complete: Superintendent Beverley Archer needed to be told.

By the time the DI was getting into bed her alarm was due to sound out in just over three hours. That would be enough sleep, she hoped, but when sleep did come it wasn't peaceful or refreshing, and she woke with a worse feeling in the base of her belly than the one she'd gone to bed with.

Back in the confines of the office, Melanie was locked in a conversation with Morris when Burton arrived. She dropped her workbag off at her desk and caught an ominous 'What kind of internet searches?' from Melanie's conversation with Morris, but Burton knew it wasn't appropriate to interject with questions. Soon after her arrival, Fairer and Read arrived with Carter trailing behind them. The team had just about dropped their bags and turned on their monitors when Melanie rallied them together, herding them toward the chairs gathered in front of their interactive board. Morris stayed rooted to her own computer while she orchestrated the technology display, and once the screen kicked into life she joined the rest of the team. Burton and Carter were seated next to each other, close enough to share a concerned look as the alleged murder footage from yesterday's call-out spread across the board.

The camera focused on a man who looked to be in his mid- to late-thirties, and he was sitting – or rather, was propped up – on a wooden chair. In the background there was a spread of white wall with nothing interesting or distinctive displayed on it.

The man was the only thing on the screen for a good twenty seconds; his head lolled to one side as though he were either drunk or drugged, but he was aware enough to acknowledge another person entering the room. He angled his eyes toward what must have been an entry point, somewhere off-camera, and soon after this gesture a woman appeared. The camera was angled in such a way that only the woman's body was visible; chiselled collar bones came into view occasionally but that was as low as she got in her first seconds on-screen, as though she knew the camera would catch her.

'What's happening?' the man asked, his words heavy with sleep.

'You know what's happening,' the woman replied. In stark contrast, her voice was calm and controlled; there was no venom in her tone, which made it seem as though whatever this was, it at least wasn't an angry act.

The woman's body remained in focus as she placed a hand on each of the man's shoulders and began to paw at the skin there.

'Boss, what is this?' Fairer piped up, giving voice to the confused looks held by the rest of the team.

'You'll find out soon enough, Brian, just bloody watch it,' Burton snapped before the DI could.

On-screen the woman leaned forward, as though reaching for the camera, but her hand settled to the right of the screen. She pulled back a glass with two inches of liquid left inside and held it close to the man's face.

'Can you drink the rest of this for me?' she asked, and the man replied with a slow nod. He was clearly in no position to give consent to anything, but she accepted this gesture as enough. She guided his head back and flicked once at his bottom lip to get him to open his mouth, before she slowly poured in the rest of the drink. When she leaned forward to put the empty glass back, the camera jerked once and the screen cut out.

It took three seconds for the footage to kick back into life and the same man as before was on-screen, now notably more dosed up than he had been. His head lolled back at an angle that looked unnatural, and he held this position until the woman came to stand behind him. The back of his head was propped against the flat of her stomach; a stretch of visible skin between the end of the woman's jeans and the start of her pale-yellow T-shirt. There was nothing exciting or extraordinary about her appearance from what could be seen.

She placed her hands on the man's shoulder again, pressing hard into them with whitening fingers as though she were feeling for something. Whatever she was looking for, she'd found it this second time.

'I think we're okay now,' she said, still feeling at his shoulders and then his neck.

'We're,' the man started, but stopped to slap his lips together. 'We're okay now,' he managed, although it didn't sound like a question so much as a confirmation of the woman's own assessment. 'We're okay now,' he said again, as her hands moved from his shoulders back to the sides of his neck. From the camera angle, it was easy to spot her fingertips feeling their way along him, pressing into his skin, shifting muscle as they went along. 'We're okay now,' he said again, quieter than before.

'Ssh, you're right. We're okay now.'

In a swift movement she placed one hand over the lower part of his face and another over the middle region, cutting off airways to his nose and mouth – and then the struggle started. The man's head knocked back against the woman, landing against the soft of her stomach, but she held on firm. With knuckles whitening, she appeared to apply additional force to his face as he pushed back against her, as though she were using his resistance to her advantage. The man shifted his head from side to side in jerked movements; a snap shift left then right as though he might shake her off. But this last kick of energy seemed to help her. Seconds later, her hands still planted firmly across his face, his head snapped back again to hit her stomach as a convulsion started. The taut body of the man tremored, jolted – and then stopped.

The woman kept her hands in place for a second or two longer before letting them fall to the man's chest. They rested there, as though waiting for the rise and fall of his breathing, but when nothing came she stepped away from the body.

'Thank you for this,' she said, to someone off-screen perhaps? But there was no evidence that anyone else was present. She hovered for a few seconds longer before stepping out of frame, and then the screen cut to black.

6

Superintendent Archer closed the laptop as the video ended. Melanie was sitting opposite her superior; she'd declined to watch the video for a second time that day. Archer rested her elbows on the edge of her desk and propped her head inside her hands for a second, before rubbing hard at her eyes with the ball of each palm, as though she might rub away what she'd seen. She eventually dropped back into the support of her chair and met Melanie's eyes.

'How many people have seen this?' she asked.

'Me, the team, George Waller.'

'Outside the station?'

'There's no way of knowing,' Melanie admitted, with a tone rich in disappointment. 'I've got Fairer and Read going back to the school where it came from to interview the kids who have seen it. We should know more before the end of the working day.'

'Christ.' Archer leaned forward again. 'Do we know who the victim is?'

'No, but we might have an idea for finding out. Morris has suggested isolating a still of the victim from the first portion of the video, which we can officially distribute with the strapline that the man is a person of interest in an ongoing investigation.' This was one thing at least that Melanie could deliver with some confidence; it was a good idea from her team, but the superintendent didn't seem convinced. 'If you'd rather we didn't, ma'am–'

'No, no it's not that.' The other woman cut across her. 'I've never known anything like it, Watton, that's all.'

'That seems to be the most common reaction so far.'

'We're certain? We're absolutely bloody certain that this is what it looks like?' She leaned further forward as she spoke, her elbows sliding across the desk an extra inch to lessen the gap between her and Melanie.

'Waller said he's as sure as he can be without having a body.'

Archer held her silence for a disconcerting stretch of time. Melanie had never seen her superior so rattled by something; although her team had reacted in a similar way too. The DI was about to highlight further benefits to their plan when her superior shared her own thoughts.

'Okay, get Morris on to it. Before you release anything to the media, make missing persons your first stop. Take the picture, give them the ongoing investigation spin. I don't want the truth of this outside of your department, do you understand?'

Melanie gave a curt nod of agreement before thanking her senior and stepping out of the office. She power-walked back through the corridors and up the stairs to her team's shared space, ready to press on with distributing orders. However, when she pushed back the door she saw there was no need to get anyone onto anything. Morris already had a copy of the video up on her screen; meanwhile Carter and Burton were hunched around a computer monitor, the former reading things aloud while the latter was taking notes. The only officer who appeared to be at a loose end was Read, who soon stepped up to greet his boss.

'Brian is on the phone to the school,' he said, nodding to his partner two desks away. 'He's trying to arrange for a meeting with the kids this afternoon, so we don't lose the weekend.'

'That's great, Read, good work.'

'Oi, chap!' Fairer shouted seconds later. 'Get your coat, you've pulled.'

'Is that sexual harassment in the workplace?' Read batted back to his partner as he walked to his desk to collect his coat and badge. 'We'll keep you in the loop over the afternoon, boss,' he reassured Melanie as both officers headed toward the door.

With the two of them on their travels, Morris was Melanie's next stop on the tour around the room. She stepped up beside the DC and surveyed the contents of her computer screen; there was a copy of the video in one corner surrounded by small tiles that looked to be shots captured from various points of the footage.

'How did you know we'd get permission for this?' Melanie asked, her tone light.

Morris turned to face her superior. 'Was there another option for getting things off the ground?' She looked back at her monitor and finished isolating one last frame before she fell back in her chair and took a hard look at their options. 'Some of these are going to be more public-friendly than others,' she announced as Melanie pulled up a chair to sit down next to her. One by one, Morris clicked on the images she'd managed to steal from the footage. She was four pictures in when she said: 'This is the best one, I think, which is the last I managed to take before she gave him the rest of whatever was in that glass.'

The two officers looked through the rest of the images, but Melanie found herself in agreement with Morris' first choice.

'Can you run off a copy of that?' Melanie asked, and Morris set about clicking her way through to print.

'Will media need more than one hard copy?'

'It's not going to media yet, it's going to missing persons. Can you email a digital copy to Carter and Burton?'

At the sound of their names, the two detectives appeared from behind the computer monitor that shielded them.

'What are you two doing behind there?' Melanie asked, crossing the room.

'Edd has been reading about snuff films, I've been writing down whatever might be useful to us,' Burton explained, flashing her boss two A4 sheets of paper that were littered with small boxes of notes that Chris had fenced off. 'There's a lot of information about these things out there.'

'Information we can use?' Melanie asked.

'It turns out there are no snuff films,' Carter interjected. 'It's an urban myth but the proof of one ever really existing is tenuous at best. Are we sure about this, boss? Like, are we sure this is actually what it looks like?'

Melanie rubbed a hand over her face as though washing clean her expression. 'Do you want to call Waller and have it out with him?'

Carter shot a look at Burton before looking back at the DI. 'No, boss, I do not.'

Morris appeared then and passed the printed image over the top of the monitor. Carter took it from her and gave it a good look over.

'You know, if you're hoping that the internet will be of use then you need to look over the dark web, or the deep web, actually. That'll be more help than anything else with something like this,' Morris said, her tone neutral. Her three fellow officers all turned on her with shared confusion. 'It's part of the internet–'

'But we're on the internet,' Carter interrupted.

'Yes, but you don't have the right software to be on the dark part of the internet,' Morris replied, her tone curter than it had been before the interruption. 'I haven't had the chance to talk any of them through it yet,' she added, speaking directly to Melanie. 'On one of my away days with the technology team they talked us through the distinction between dark and deep web, how to search through them, that sort of thing.'

'So, this is familiar territory for you?' Melanie asked.

'I mean, I'm no rookie.' Morris glanced at Carter. 'But I'm not part of the JOC either.'

'Joint Operations Cell? This is their territory?' Burton asked, and Morris nodded in reply.

Melanie thought for a second before she said, 'Carter, take that image down to missing persons, would you?'

He stood to attention. 'Did I do something in particular to deserve this duty?'

'Many, many things, but you'll find out what they are in your performance report,' Melanie replied, her lips curling into a smile as she finished. 'Don't tell them anything; the official party-line is this man is a person of interest for an ongoing investigation and that is all you give them. Are we clear?'

'Clear. Burton?' Carter glanced down at his partner who was still seated.

'Burton stays here,' Melanie added. 'Morris is going to teach us everything we need to know about this dark web business.'

7

There was a long-standing animosity between the missing persons department and Melanie's major incident team, dating back to when a member of missing persons deliberately withheld information relating to the copycat case last year. Whenever a member of MIT needed to approach them these days there was always a coin toss to see which detective would get the duty. Carter felt the tiniest bit scorned that he hadn't been afforded that courtesy.

He pushed the door open to the department with a measured amount of caution and peered across the quiet of the office. There were one or two people he recognised but one or two people he didn't. Carter thought, in the interest of getting this over with as soon as possible, involving fresh blood might be the best option.

'Excuse me?' he asked, catching the attention of a young female officer sitting on the outskirts of the room. She turned to face Carter and there wasn't a flicker of recognition on her face, which at least reassured him they really hadn't met before. 'I was wondering whether you might be able to help me with something. I'm upstairs, from the major incident team. We're looking for a person of interest in one of our cases.'

'Sounds exciting.' The young woman stood and extended a hand. 'DC Rosa Linden, how can I help?'

Carter had to hold back a sigh of relief. He lifted the printed still from his side. 'Any chance anyone matching this chap's description has been flagged on your radar?'

'We can certainly take a look,' she said, sitting back down at her desk. She pulled her keyboard closer. 'Is he a suspect for something?'

'No, nothing so interesting. Like I said, just a person of interest.'

The woman fell quiet and clicked her way through a number of boxes at such a speed, Carter stood no chance of verifying what each screen was for. She paused on one screen to type in quick bursts, and she looked to the photograph and back between every entry, so at least Carter could understand this part of inputting the information. Although another series of screens followed, that left him lost.

'Is there a lot to sort through?' he asked.

Before the other officer could reply there was a high-pitched ping from the computer that pulled her attention to it. Her shoulders dropped. 'Nothing at all to sort through.' She turned to face Carter then. 'It doesn't look like we've got any hits. I can scan this in though,' she added, looking at the image. 'If anything comes in, I can call.'

When Fairer and Read arrived at the school, the head teacher met them at the entranceway. The formal introductions were made before the woman cut straight to business, and both detectives would later admit they were impressed with her organisational skills. She led them through the corridors of the school, all the while narrating the events of the hour and a half that had passed since they called to arrange a visit.

'Damien Fuller was the young man who blew the whistle on the whole thing but I haven't been able to contact his parents, and I can't allow you to speak to him without their permission,' she said, coming to a halt outside of a closed classroom. 'The boys who were passing around the offending article are all in here, though, and I have emails from their parents granting you permission to speak to them, providing I remain present. I hope that won't be a problem?'

This was the easiest access they'd ever been granted. 'That suits us entirely, Dr Oakley, thank you for being so efficient about this,' Read replied.

'Anything to help.'

Dr Oakley pushed into the room and an immediate silence fell over the three boys who were seated inside. She introduced them one by one – Aiden Harris, Benjamin Castle, and Rhys Wilkins – and each boy turned ashen as they came face to face with the detectives. They were given instructions to comply with the officers' questions before Dr Oakley slipped out of their eyelines and came to a rest against the back wall of the room. But from the boys' expressions it was clear her presence was still felt.

'Benjamin Castle, you're the young man who had this footage on his phone, right?' Fairer started, sitting down near the boy. Benji nodded but it looked as though the admission pained him. 'You're not in trouble, lad, we just want to know where it came from. Was it someone else in the school who sent it?' Fairer shot a pointed look at the other two as he asked this question.

'No.' Benji spoke into the desk. 'It came from outside of school.'

'So, are you the one who sent it around the school?' Read cut in.

Benji nodded again. 'I didn't think anything of it; it was just a stupid film.'

'It's not like we were sending around anything dirty,' Rhys Wilkins added. 'That would have been worse, right?' he asked the detectives before turning to face the head teacher. 'Dr Oakley, wouldn't that have been worse?'

'I think it would have been better than engaging in a criminal act,' Read added before the head could respond. Fairer and Read had decided which one of them would be friendly and which one firm during the drive to the school.

'So, it's real then?' Aiden Harris spoke for the first time.

'We're still trying to verify whether it's real or not,' Fairer replied.

'But you think it might be?'

'Mr Harris, we're not at liberty to divulge information, and we're actually here to ask you the questions,' Read snapped, and the young man dropped his head to face the desk again. 'We already know Benjamin Castle has footage of the recording. Do you two have it as well?'

'They did,' Dr Oakley added from the back of the room. 'The phones are now in a locked drawer in my office.'

'How many people did you send it to, Benjamin?' Fairer asked, his tone still soft.

The boy shrugged. 'I really don't know, I'm sorry. These two.' He nodded to his friends. 'A few others, as well, I think.'

'Inside the school?'

'And at different schools,' Benjamin admitted, with a shake to his voice.

'What about you two?' Fairer asked. 'How many people have you sent it to by now?'

'A few, I suppose.'

'A few for me too, I think,' Rhys agreed.

'Can you let us know the names of the schools this is making its way around now, Benjamin?' Read asked, and the boy nodded in quiet agreement. 'What're the chances of you telling us the names of students who sent it to you while you're at it?' A determined silence fell over the kid then, and he held his eye contact with the desk. 'We're not going to hammer down their door, Benjamin, but we do need to know where this started, and you'd be helping us a lot with the investigation.'

Fairer spotted the subtle headshake from the lad as he resisted questioning for a final time; they didn't have the time or the authority to stay here and crack a teenager.

'Thanks for your time, gentlemen,' Fairer said as he made for the door. Read offered no such farewell, but instead shot the lads a cutting look, laying the ground for whatever interviews might come next.

'I'm sorry that they couldn't be, or rather wouldn't be, of more use,' Dr Oakley said when the three of them were a safe distance from the room. 'I can get the names of the other schools from Benjamin this afternoon and see that they're forwarded on to you. Should I notify the other head teachers?'

'That won't be necessary,' Read replied, his tone still curt from questioning.

'If you can send them over at your earliest convenience, we'll see they're notified before the day is out,' Fairer added. 'If we could grab the handsets from you as well, that would be great.'

'Of course, detective, my office is through here.'

Read remained frosty through his goodbyes with the head teacher and through the journey back to the station. He was glad the interview had been relatively pain-free, but he wished they could take back better news than details of how far-spread this horror could soon become...

8

Carter leaned against the open doorway of his bathroom and watched his daughter brush her teeth after breakfast. It filled him with a sincere contentment to have his daughter back under the same roof as him. He'd picked her up from Trish's on the way home from work and they'd spent a long evening talking about school and playground antics, but it was the perfect antidote after the last few days.

'I'm finished, Dad,' Emily said, stepping down from the small stool that allowed her access to the bathroom mirror. She still hadn't had another growth spurt.

Carter crouched down level with his daughter. 'Let me see?'

'Aaaaahhhhh,' Emily said, her mouth stretched wide. They collapsed into a small huddle of laughter, each of them making overblown 'Aaaaahhhh' noises between giggles. It was the happiest Carter had been since his last time with Emily. He was on weekends with her, which meant missing out on overtime, but it seemed a fair trade.

~

The station was unnervingly quiet. Melanie scanned herself through to the inner sanctum and climbed the stairs to her office. Morris had set Melanie up with dark web access before the end of play yesterday and, despite her promises not to get drawn into the online playground too soon, Melanie needed to feel like she was doing something. She soon saw that it was a shared feeling when she pushed open the door to the communal office space to find Burton and Morris already in cahoots around a computer screen. Both officers snapped around at the sound of an intruder and visibly softened when they spotted their superior.

'Morning, boss,' Morris chirped.

'You two don't have better things to do?'

'Actually, we don't,' Burton replied, and Morris nodded in agreement.

'Okay, what angle are you taking?' Melanie asked, pulling up a seat alongside them. Burton gestured for Morris to take the floor.

'With the tech team I've been looking at digital footprints; simple enough idea, anywhere you go online you leave a footprint to say you've been there. I'm wondering whether there's a way to track digital footprints from anything left behind on the video.' She paused to gesture to what looked like strings of computer code, spread out across her monitor. 'The video has a back end just like anything else, a list of properties and authors, it's just a bit of a mess because it's been sent around so much.'

'So, it's been sent around to more than just a handful of viewers?' Melanie cut in.

Morris appeared deflated. 'That's about the only thing we've managed to spot so far, yes. I'm hoping I'll find a way to pick up something more specific by looking through the different handles that are attached to the file now; there will be something, boss, I just – I don't know how long it's going to take to find.'

Melanie stared at the foreign writings on the screen in front of her, lost in thought somewhere. 'This is really good stuff, Morris, stick with it,' she eventually said before she turned to Burton. 'Are you helping out with this, or have you got your own sideline?'

'I came in to watch the video again. It sounds morbid, but I was hoping that once we'd got used to the whole murder thing, we might be able to spot something other than, you know...' Chris trailed off and finished the sentence with a down-pulled expression. 'But if you'd rather I didn't?'

'It sounds smart, Burton, as long as you can stomach it. If you can't, you can help me; I'll be in my office learning everything I can about snuff films.' Melanie stood as she spoke. 'If you need anything or find anything,' she said, before pointing to her office. She left her junior officers to their work and, as she stepped through into her private office space, Melanie braced herself for whatever it was she was about to find.

Nearly three hours had passed when Burton reached in to knock against Melanie's open door. She gestured for Burton to take a seat and she did so.

'Lucy and I are going to get something to eat; can you drag yourself away?' she asked.

Melanie rubbed hard at her eyes. 'It's like a car crash, you know?' she said, and Burton nodded in understanding. 'I don't even know what I'm looking for. It started off with snuff films but there have been tangential trips down drug smuggling and bitcoin avenues. I don't feel like I've found anything to help with this case so much as I have found twenty other cases we could follow up on, which makes me even more nervous that we should be involving another department.' Melanie slammed her laptop closed with a force that made Burton jump. 'Sorry, Chris, it's just – Jesus, where do you even start? We don't have a body, or a crime scene, or a killer, despite having her on tape–'

'We have dead air,' Morris interrupted from the open doorway.

Burton turned to face her colleague. 'Excuse me?'

This at least made Morris smile. 'You asked me to enhance the sound on the recording,' she continued, stepping into the office and bringing a small laptop with her. She set it down on the desk between the other two officers before adding, 'Chris thought we might find a link through whoever the woman is talking to.'

'Whoever she thanks?' Melanie clarified and Morris held a thumb up in confirmation.

'I've spotted minor things on the video so far. There are screws in the wall where something should be, for instance. I think it's a domestic building, but that doesn't give us much to go with. My other idea was that we might get audio traces of someone else on the recording,' Burton explained.

'So we'd at least know whether the accomplice was male or female,' Morris added, and it was clear from their complementary sentences that the two had really put their heads together for this one. 'Chris asked me if I could amplify the sound to find another voice somewhere,' she said, hitting a button that triggered the video to start up.

The three women leaned in closer to the machine and listened to the whirring of internal parts, matched by the crisp silence of absolutely nothing taking place on the video. Then came the woman's final line – 'Thank you for this.' – but there was nothing to accompany it; no breathing, no movement.

'Nothing at all?' Melanie asked as the video closed.

'Absolutely nothing. I've ramped this up as much as I can. I can ask someone on the external team to try to do something more with it, but I really don't see that there's anything else sound-wise, boss.'

'Who is she thanking then? If not someone else, then who?' Melanie snapped without meaning to, but the revelation was an uncomfortable and disappointing one. Morris kept quiet although she was clearly as thrown as Melanie, that much was apparent from the DC's expression. Cutting through the silence that seemed to last a beat too long, Burton, using one of her quieter tones, finally proffered a suggestion: 'Him? I think she must be thanking him.'

9

One by one the officers filtered into the office on Monday morning. Carter was the last to arrive, a smile on his face and a grease stain on the collar of his shirt, because Emily had hugged him while eating her toast. He set his work gear down by his desk before heading straight into Melanie's office to get caught up on the weekend's action. Carter knocked at the half-open door and pushed through into the space to find Melanie already wrapped up in a phone call. She gestured for him to take a seat and he did so, half-listening as he waited for her to finish.

'Yes, ma'am, I understand that.'

From her tone and her phrasing, Carter knew it must be Archer she was speaking to.

'Yes, whenever you have the time to. ... Carter is in front of me right now, so I can arrange for that when we're finished. ... Thank you, ma'am, yes, absolutely.'

Melanie dropped the phone onto her desk and buried her face in her open palms.

'What have we got ourselves into?' she said, her voice muffled as she spoke into her hands. She looked up at Carter and flashed a tight smile. 'Missing persons didn't get in touch yet, so could you chase them today? I don't trust them to be forthcoming with information.'

'Of course, I'll make it my first job after briefing.'

'Over the weekend Morris got me started on the dark web but truthfully, I don't know what I'm looking for. Her and Burton worked on the video over the weekend too and they've got a theory about who the woman was speaking to, or maybe wasn't speaking to. I'll explain in the briefing, it'll save you hearing it twice,' she said, waving the rest of her explanation away.

It wasn't a thought worth sharing but Carter couldn't help but feel irked; firstly, that Burton had beaten him to the punch on extra time and secondly, that he was being told things at the same meeting as everyone else. It was childish, he knew, but a perk of his rank had always been the insider knowledge.

'We've got time before the briefing,' Melanie started again, double-checking her watch. 'Do you mind heading down to missing persons now?'

Carter nodded. 'Of course. Don't start without me, will you?'

Melanie didn't seem to notice the pointed comment, but simply murmured in agreement.

The team were gathered into their usual seats for the briefing and Carter took his place at the front of the room; which at least did something to ease his earlier discomfort. He eyed his superior as she prepared to address the squad. She looked tired, stressed, and it wasn't a good sign to see her so worked up this early on in a case. There was nothing good coming, Carter realised.

'Okay, this video,' Melanie started, calling the group's attention. 'Morris and Burton spent some time with it over the weekend to try to isolate another person in the background anywhere, someone our killer might have been speaking to.'

'Is this for the "thank you" comment?' Read clarified.

'Bingo. Burton thought we might find traces of another person, breathing or movement of some kind. Audio enhancement shows nothing; there's no audible sign of another individual being in that room with them.'

'So, who's she thanking?' Fairer asked, in a tone that suggested he was waiting for a good punchline.

Melanie shrugged. 'That's the question, isn't it?' She turned to write on the whiteboard behind her then, *Who does the killer speak to?*, before picking up with the rest of the update. 'Our working theory is that she's thanking the victim, but we need to know more about this tape before we can draw any real conclusions.' She paused for a beat to allow for questions. 'Morris has also set me up on the dark web and I've been looking through details pertaining to snuff films, and drug smuggling and organ selling,' she said, her tone frustrated. 'I've found a good two dozen reasons to alert joint operations cell to what we're doing, but nothing at all relating to our own case.'

Carter's ears pricked up. He'd heard of the joint operations cell before, how the team was put together specifically to handle crime on the dark web. They were a well-known organisation to police teams up and down the country. But Carter never thought he'd have the chance to actually work with them.

'Is that a real possibility?' Read asked.

Melanie let her shoulders droop. 'It's six of one and half a dozen of the other on whether we bring them in at this stage. If we find something explicitly relating to the murder, then yes, we'll have to let them know. If we don't find anything relating to the murder, then we might have to go cap in hand for help anyway.'

'But wouldn't they want a case like this?'

'Your guess is as good as mine, Read.' Melanie tried to shake the despondency from her voice before she spoke again. 'Either way, I haven't found much yet, but Burton will be taking over with this from today.' She looked to Burton for a plan of action and she leapt at the opportunity to speak.

'I'm going to start off by reading through forums. Morris and I spoke over the weekend and we thought if people are going to plan a snuff film, it might be they're talking to other people with similar interests?' Burton directed the intonation toward Morris who gave a nod of agreement. 'I'll isolate relevant forums and do a specific search for snuff and associated terms.'

'Okay, and while you're doing that, Carter, what luck have we had chasing up our victim as a missing person?' Melanie asked, switching her attention.

'None at all, boss. I spoke to DC Linden and she said that nothing was flagged up over the weekend. She'll raise any possibilities with us, but nothing to report for now.'

'That settles it, then.' Melanie recapped the pen and a took a seat at the front of the group. 'Carter and I will be speaking at a press conference toward the end of today, if that suits you, Edd?' She paused for his confirmation, and Carter felt a wave of relief that she'd asked. 'The superintendent is putting things in place. We'll be releasing the image with the same party-line that we've used so far; he's a person of interest in an ongoing investigation. But we need to ramp up the gears on this, folks. Searching for a killer is one thing, but a missing body is something else.'

Melanie spent the morning in her office talking through strategies with Carter. It proved harder than expected to form a line of enquiry around a missing victim, without admitting that was who their person of interest was. The pair tried on various reworkings of the truth until Melanie eventually tired of the boyish excitement that came along with each suggestion Carter made.

'You're enjoying this far too much,' Melanie said.

Carter looked taken aback. 'I have no idea what you're talking about.'

'No? You're not the tiniest bit excited about all this?' She gestured somewhere beyond the room, to their worker bee colleagues who were piecing evidence together. 'You're like a kid in a goddamn sweet shop, Carter, and you need to can it.'

'Mel, c'mon–'

'I'm being serious.'

The harsh tap of knuckles against the door came as a welcome interruption. Burton stepped into the office with the caution of a child interrupting their arguing parents.

'Bad timing?' she said.

'Perfect timing,' Melanie replied. 'What have you got?'

'A young man in the station who claims to have information about the video.' Melanie shot from her seat and crossed the room while Burton continued. 'Apparently he's the older brother of one of the boys from the school, and he thinks he'll be able to help us.'

Carter joined the two women in the doorway. 'What are we waiting for?'

'You're staying here,' Melanie replied. Carter parted his mouth to dispute the order, but he didn't get further than an opening puff of air. 'What did I literally just say to you, Carter? We have a press conference before the day is out.'

'I can prep for the conference if Carter wants to take point on this?' Burton intervened, but Melanie turned on her with a glare. 'Or not.'

'Lead the way, Burton, you're sitting in with me on this.'

Melanie followed Burton out the room, leaving Carter to

stare down a sheet full of notes, a pack full of printouts, and very few ideas to work with.

'Did I miss something?' Burton asked, walking level with her superior.

Melanie sighed. 'Carter is uncomfortably close to being a glory-chaser after just one grubby case. He's better than that.'

'He's going through things.'

'What, a divorce?'

'Well, yeah.'

'Please.' Melanie huffed as she pushed through the first set of double doors down to the station. 'He's lucky he's got someone in his life that he can go through divorce proceedings with.' From Burton's expression it was clear that Melanie had crossed a line and she didn't know what her chances were of hopping back over it. 'The lads are hard work sometimes, that's all. It's like herding cats between them.'

Burton cracked a smile. 'Still, try not to step on too many tails.' The women shared a softened look. 'The chaps can get their feelings hurt too, that's all I'm saying.'

Burton pushed through into reception and held the door open for her superior. There, loitering around the empty space was a six foot-something male who, if Melanie had to guess, was twenty-two, perhaps twenty-three, years of age. He looked like the kind of young man who might be dragged into the station on a Saturday night, rather than the type who would elect to make an appearance here.

'Excuse me.' The desk sergeant wrangled the attention of the man. 'Sir, these are the officers you're looking for.' He pointed to Melanie and Burton as he spoke.

Melanie stepped toward the visitor with a hand outstretched and the gesture appeared to throw the young man as he approached her. Nevertheless, he shared a nervous handshake before introducing himself.

'I'm Ricky Castle.'

Melanie thought. 'Benjamin's brother?' The young man nodded. 'You heard about the tape through the trouble at the school?'

'Sort of.' He paused and rubbed at the back of his neck. 'I'm the one who sent it.'

'Burton,' Melanie spoke from the side of her mouth, unwilling to take her eyes off the man in front of her.

'On it.' Burton closed the distance between herself and the desk sergeant. 'Any chance of an interview room?'

'I assume you're happy to have a talk with us?' Melanie clarified.

'Happy might be a push.' He laughed; Melanie didn't. 'Yes, completely. I want to help.'

'If you want to follow me this way?' Burton interrupted, heading toward the corridor that housed the interview rooms, complete with camera and audio feeds.

Melanie gestured for the young man to follow her colleague. Castle held up his silence while he was sandwiched in between the officers, but no sooner had they taken their seats and information spilled from him like beans from an upended coffee jar.

'I only sent it to him because I thought it was fake. I obviously wouldn't have sent it if I'd known what it was; if I'd known that it was real.'

'So, you believe it's real?' Melanie's own tone was measured, calm.

He looked from one officer to the other. 'I mean, isn't it?'

Melanie shot Burton an encouraging look before she leaned back in her chair.

'To clarify a couple of things, I'm DC Burton and this is DI Watton. We're both part of the team who are currently investigating the file, or rather the contents of the file, and we're therefore not at liberty to discuss details pertaining to that ongoing investigation.' The information rushed from Burton as though she were mentally ticking off boxes. Melanie had to hold back on a smile. 'Before we go any further, can you confirm your name for us? This conversation is being recorded, so we need to make you aware of that.' She gestured to the camera that was tucked into a corner somewhere behind her.

'Ricky Castle,' the young man replied. He leaned forward and lowered his head as he spoke, as though there was a microphone feed woven into the table.

'And you've seen the contents of the footage?'

'Yes.'

'Where did you get this footage?'

Ricky rubbed a palm over his closely shaved head. 'A friend sent it to me.'

'Does this friend have a name?'

'It's hard to say.'

'The name is hard to say, or it's hard to say who the friend is?' Melanie couldn't help herself. 'Mr Castle, you led us to believe that you had new information regarding the tape.'

'Jesus, okay. I don't want Benji being in trouble for something that I sent him.' His hands were spread flat on the table, as though he were trying to steady himself. 'My friend Liam sent it to me, but I know that our mate Felix sent it to him. I don't know who sent it to him but I'd guess that it was our friend Tess, because that's the sort of thing she's into.' Melanie's eyes widened. 'Oh fuck, no, not like... not like *into*.' Ricky faltered and clenched his fists before speaking again. 'She's into special effects and that's why I'd guess that she's the one who it came from, but you'd need to speak to them all to be certain because really it could have come from anywhere.'

This wasn't the information Melanie had been hoping for, and from the heavy sigh that escaped Burton, Melanie knew it was a shared disappointment.

'Can you give us contact details for these people?' Burton asked. She reached inside her pocket and pulled out a notebook. 'Any contact details at all would be useful.' She encouraged the witness, but he seemed stumped by the request.

'Is there a problem?' Melanie pushed.

'No. But I mean, what are you hoping for?' Ricky blurted. 'Because, like, anyone can find this footage, right? It's out there now. That's what I wanted to tell you. Like, I can't tell you where it came from; I can only tell you where Benji's copy came from because I sent it to him and...' Ricky's explanation petered out when he spotted Melanie's expression.

'Take down anything that could be useful, would you?' Melanie spoke directly to Burton. 'Mr Castle, thank you for your time.' She pushed back from the table and excused herself. The young man had been given enough of her civilities, Melanie reasoned, as she powered back through the station toward her own floor of the building.

When Melanie pushed her way into the shared office space, she spotted Carter had resumed his position at his own desk. He was staring at his monitor with such an intensity that he didn't seem to notice Melanie had arrived until she was standing in front of him.

'Carter, I pray to God that you've got something for me because that arse took an hour of life that I won't get back.' She was firm, but her tone was notably more friendly than it had been earlier, and from Carter's expression she thought he'd noticed.

'Well, do I have the thing for you.' He felt around on his desk for something before settling on a green Post-it note. He pinned the small square to the edge of the desk for Melanie to inspect. 'It might not be an ID, boss, but it's certainly a line of enquiry.'

10

Morris hit *complete download* as it appeared in the corner of her colleague's screen and she waited until the installation started before she stood. Read hovered alongside her, looking over her shoulder at intervals. When the installation was near completion along its progress bar, Morris clicked her way through a series of commands and expelled a hard sigh as she felt part of her colleague's leg press against her own – again. He had been peering over her shoulder for the duration of the download and Morris was sick of the supervision.

'Read,' she started, turning to face him. 'Can you do this on your own?'

'I mean, it's a download, how hard can it be?'

'Cool, I'll leave you to finish this off then.'

Morris sidestepped her colleague and powered back to her own desk where she landed hard on her chair. Burton and Fairer swapped amused looks over the tops of their monitors as a collection of confused clicks arose from Read's desk. The frantic clicking was soon followed by an unimpressed sound from the speaker system.

'Doing alright there, lad?' Fairer said.

'Doing fine, it's this bloody thing that's the problem.' Read back-stepped from the computer, as though putting a safe distance between himself and it. 'It's saying the download has failed and I haven't even done anything.'

'You didn't click anything?' Burton spoke through the beginnings of a laugh.

'Fuck sake.' Morris pushed herself away from her desk space with a hard shove. 'If you hadn't touched anything, it would have finished downloading on its own.' She crossed the space between her desk and Read's. Her colleague held a strong silence while Morris bent down to inspect the string of messages that were displayed across the screen. There came a stammer of clicks as she remedied the issues. Then she stood upright, again, and instructed her colleague, again, 'I'll leave you to finish this off then.' She turned back for one final reminder, 'Don't touch a thing on that computer.'

Since the press conference had taken place two days ago there had been an influx of maybe-identifications from members of the public who sort-of-recognised the man in the image. But nothing concrete had come about despite Melanie's pleas for information, using Carter's strapline that the man was wanted for questioning in relation to a new pornography ring. 'I know it's not porn,' Carter explained, 'but it's close enough, surely?' Melanie had had to agree, despite the guilty shift in her innards as she approved it. There were one or two interesting calls that Melanie and Carter had followed up but then dismissed, which left the team with no other option but to start exploring other areas of interest – namely, the dark web.

'What are we even looking for here?' Fairer erupted.

Burton sighed. 'You know what we're looking for; anything that looks like a snuff film.'

'Or someone talking about a snuff film,' Morris added.

'You know what a snuff film is, right, Brian?' Carter interjected, his tone jovial as he emerged from Melanie's office, with the DI trailing behind him. 'You're looking for anything that looks like it could be useful to us, starting with anyone who is talking snuff, or talking about making it. Right, boss?' He turned to face Melanie who was leaning in her open doorway.

'Right, and from the blank expressions, I'm guessing we're not there yet?'

'Read, have you got anything?' Burton added with a smirk.

Melanie was in her office ordering a takeaway for the team – who were in their fourth hour of searching and their first hour of overtime – when she heard Fairer holler from the outside office. 'Folks, folks, I might have something here.'

The team rushed to congregate around the officer's monitor, making way for Melanie as she arrived. She crouched down to gain a better view of the screen and asked, 'What are we dealing with, Fairer?'

'There's a forum about sex tapes that I fell into. People were talking about inappropriate stuff; you know, illegal stuff,' he said the words softly, as though they might be hard for people to hear. 'Someone said they were looking at lots of near-death experiences, and then this one user appears from nowhere...'

Snuffmegood:
```
What about snuff films
Are people into those yet
```

'Snuff me good?' Carter repeated. 'Isn't that someone on the receiving end of it?'

'What, like our mystery man?' Melanie said, her tone flat. 'Keep going, Fairer.'

Bookmebookyou:
Far cry from near-death man
Snuff doesn't even exist though
Am I right
Collarforadollar:
Everything exists when you know where to look
Am I right
Snuffmegood:
Okay
What if I were looking to make a snuff
Anyone here for that
Killmequick:
Here for it how
Are you on top or below

'I don't even know what that means in this context,' Read interrupted, and there was a grunt of agreement from someone in the huddle.

Edd sighed. 'You know, who's doing, who's being done.'

Melanie ignored the comments and encouraged Fairer to continue scrolling.

Hotforheels:
Oh come on
Who actually wants to die
Who actually wants to kill someone

'Most of the conversation carries on between these players here for a while,' Fairer noted, clicking through the continued exchanges that seemed to stretch for reams. 'But then when we get down here – we're hours into their talk by this stage, if you look at the timestamps for everything – this user appears.' He pointed to the screen as he spoke to isolate the new speaker. 'Domdomdom.'

'Like, dom?' Burton repeated. As though catching the confused look from her DI, she added, 'I mean, dom like dominant, dominatrix, or dom like...' she faltered.

'A dramatic reveal?' Carter suggested. 'You know, dun dun dun.'

Domdomdom:
I'm game if people are talking snuff
Greysgotnothing:
Honey please, who would actually
Snuffmegood:
I would actually
Domdomdom:
Then why don't we take this private

'That's the beginning and end of it,' Fairer said, with an aggressive spin of his mouse wheel. 'There's no mention of snuff again, no appearance from this Dom character in the forum, not that I can see at least.' He paused to rub a hand over his forehead and back through his hair. 'I don't think the other user, this snuff me good bloke, makes another appearance either.' He gave in with a defeated shrug.

'Morris?' Melanie started.

'I'll see what I can do.' She hopped desks back to her own workstation while delivering instructions to her colleague. 'I'm going to need you to double-click that forum entry and send it over to me, okay, Fairer? That's all I need, the link to it,' she said, with the same care she'd taken when giving instructions to Read earlier in the day. 'Boss, if the private chats are encrypted then there might not be a whole lot I can do here.'

'What does that mean, "if they're encrypted"? Can't we

access them how we would any other chatroom?' Carter asked, his tone mirroring Burton's confused expression as the pair came to stand together alongside Morris' desk.

'It isn't that simple,' Morris said.

'I can't see a court order helping us much when it comes to conversations like this, Carter,' Melanie added. 'Besides, it might not be our problem for much longer.'

'Why, what are you thinking?' Carter asked.

'We have good reason to believe the murder we're investigating is linked to characters who are using the dark web. At this stage, I don't think we've got another option but to let JOC know what we've found.'

'But they'll take the case,' Morris said, her voice worried at the edges.

'It's a possibility, but it'll be down to them whether they do or not when they know how much we've got.' Melanie tried to sound reassuring, unfazed. 'Do what you can in the time we've got, Morris, and keep the rest of us in the loop.' She turned to trek back to her office but Burton pulled her back around.

'What do we do in the meantime?' Burton asked.

'We've got a couple of options. You can head home and call it a night, or you can remind me what your Just Eat order was and wait it out with me and Morris,' Melanie said, and although the words themselves were playful, they landed with a flat energy.

'Righto,' Burton replied. 'Let's get on it with this food order.'

11

Their overtime was spent scrolling through the dark web. Each officer saved and printed their findings and by the following morning there were five piles of chatroom transcripts sitting on Melanie's desk. She was already part way through reading the second of them. Highlighting as she went along, she'd found talk of torture porn and bondage but she was yet to see anything that was obvious enough to relate to their snuff seekers.

Morris' search from the previous evening hadn't turned up any more information on the chatroom users; although she had managed to confirm neither of them had been active on those particular forums since they'd moved to their private chat. But perhaps they'd taken the conversation to another forum altogether. The team's best hope now, it seemed, was to find users who might be talking about their missing individuals – or at least find someone talking about this film – and that job had fallen to Melanie.

Somewhere between the second and third sets of papers, Melanie admitted defeat in tackling the case alone. She couldn't sidestep her worries that she and her team were putting themselves at risk by going head first into this online playground. She clicked through her computer to find the agency's directory and, reluctantly, she dialled through to the JOC department.

A woman with a too-chirpy voice answered. 'Good morning, you've reached the switchboard. How may I help?'

'Hi there, I'm DI Watton calling through a few case details. I've got something here pertaining to dark web dealings and I need to log the information with someone in your department.'

The woman exhaled in a near-laugh. 'JOC actually specialises in cases of that nature. Could you be more specific?'

Melanie didn't even want to be making this phone call and her patience snapped in light of that. 'We've got video footage of someone being stifled and we think it's a snuff film that may or may not have been arranged through a dark web forum.' There was a perfect silence then; Melanie couldn't even hear keys tapping. 'Is that everything you'll need?'

'DI Watton, you said?'

'Yes.'

'Someone will be in touch shortly.'

Melanie slammed the phone back into its cradle and rested her forehead in the palms of her hands, her elbows balanced on the desk. She wasn't sure she'd done the right thing, but their internet results already felt too vast, too disturbing for them. It didn't seem right not to mention them to the specialists in the field. She pushed out a heavy breath to steady herself before sitting upright. Melanie looked up in time to see a young PC coming to a stop in her doorway.

'DI Watton, there's someone downstairs who brought this in,' he said, handing over a photograph. 'He said he recognises the man from the pornography ring. He thinks it's a friend of his.' He paused and nodded to the photograph. When Melanie looked down she spotted their victim, smiling wide with a beer bottle in one hand while his other arm sat around the shoulders of another well-turned-out man of the same age. *Maybe the man who had brought the photograph in?* Melanie wondered.

'He's actually waiting downstairs,' the PC added, interrupting Melanie's focus. 'He said he'd wait in case you wanted to speak to him.'

Melanie handed the photograph back. 'Tell him I'll be right down? I need a minute.'

When the PC had exited the office Melanie quickly searched around her desk for the folder of photograph stills that Morris had pulled from the footage. They had only shared one during the press conference but there were two others that she could share, if she needed to. She removed the more sensitive ones from the collection and unlocked the bottom drawer of her desk. She knew the photos would be safe in there, protected from prying eyes. She secured the lock and dropped the key in the inside pocket of her jacket.

As Melanie pushed through the doors leading to reception she spotted the man easily; he was definitely the other person pictured. She closed the space between them and greeted him with an outstretched hand. The shift from cool office to stuffy reception had left her palm damp with sweat, but on impact she felt the warmth of the man's hand too.

'I'm DI Watton. Thanks for coming in.' The man reciprocated her welcome with a firm handshake. 'I hear you've got some information relating to our person of interest?'

'Ethan, his name is Ethan Irwill.'

So that's our victim's name, Melanie thought.

'I'm Fin Gallagher. Ethan and I are friends but I've been working up north, bit of a dead zone for signal and all the rest of it. It wasn't until I got back that another friend called me and–'

'I'm going to pause you there for a second, Mr Gallagher. Would you mind if we popped into an interview room? You're not obliged, nor are you under caution. It would just be nice for a bit of privacy to talk,' Melanie explained slowly. She was trying not to startle the man, and she was relieved to see it had worked.

Gallagher nodded and, as they both turned away from the open space of reception, the desk sergeant held up three fingers to guide Melanie toward a free interview room. She flashed a smile of thanks before heading toward the corridor, her witness trailing behind.

Melanie clicked the door closed behind them and took a seat opposite Gallagher, who was already hunched over in his chair, drumming his fingertips along the steel of the table. It was even warmer in the interview room, and Melanie wondered whether this heat was a new interrogation tactic.

Gallagher's fingers came to a stop halfway through their motion against the table as he locked eyes with Melanie. 'I'm sorry,' he explained, leaning back. 'I'm a little nervous.'

'Police stations often do that to people,' Melanie replied, in a tone that sounded harsher than she'd intended.

'Oh, it's not the station, it's just – Christ, all this business with Ethan. The news seems to think he's some sort of pornographer?'

'I can't discuss details of the case at this time.' Melanie swallowed down the desire to correct the man. 'But any information you can give us would be extremely helpful at this point in our investigation.' She drew her notebook from her inside pocket. 'You said you'd been away for a while, with work?'

'That's right. I'm an insurance investigator, nothing too glamorous, but it sends me around the country sometimes.' The man paused and narrowed his eyes at Melanie who had started to note something down. She gestured for him to continue. 'There's a group of us who usually go out drinking together at the weekend; me, Ethan, one or two others. One of the lads, when I got back last night, he said there was a bloke on the news who looked just like Ethan and I didn't think anything of it until I saw himself myself.'

'You're quite sure it's him?'

'As sure as I can be without having the man in front of me. But that's the other thing.'

Melanie was glad to see the question of work and where-abouts had loosened the man into talking; the old ones were the best.

'When I recognised the man off the news as Ethan, I tried calling him, both on his mobile and at home, and I can't get through to him.'

'And that's unusual?'

'For him, definitely. The bloody phone is fixed to his hand.'

Melanie noted down one or two further ideas as the man continued to dole out information. When he came to a natural pause, she asked, 'You'll be able to supply us with these details, I assume? Phone numbers, home address, that sort of thing?'

'Absolutely, no problem. I can even put you in touch with the lads if it'll help.'

'Thank you, that'd be useful too. Is there any family we might be able to contact?' Melanie asked, wondering why the man's drinking buddies were the first to notice something was wrong.

'Ethan's an only child. His mum passed away a few months after he'd finished uni.'

Melanie took down the details. 'I'm sorry to hear that. There's no father on the scene?'

'He's literally never mentioned his dad, so...' his speech trailed off, as though what he'd said was a complete explanation. Melanie understood; families were complicated things. But there was still something saddening about how easily Ethan seemed to have slipped away.

'The other friends you've mentioned, you think they'll be willing to have a chat?'

'Sure, of course. I just think – don't think me rude because I know it's your job and all, but there must be a mix-up somewhere along the line.' The man hesitated and ran a hand through his hair. 'I mean, Ethan, he's told us all some stories in his time but he's hardly a bloody lothario.'

Melanie felt her interest catch. 'What kind of stories?'

'You know, shit that you talk about with blokes at the pub. It was always one-upmanship with him and the others.' He thought for a second. 'And with me, too, if I'm honest about it. I've done this so he's done that; I've had two so he's had three, that sort of lark.'

Melanie blinked to avoid a hard eye-roll.

'He liked girls with a few kinks to them, you know, ones willing to try new things. Not once did he mention filming anything though and not to discredit him, but I'm sure he would have mentioned something like that.'

'It would have been a string to his bow?' Melanie's tone was flat, and Gallagher's startled expression told her that he'd noticed the hard edge of her question. 'Mr Gallagher, this has been really useful and I'm glad you've come forward. If it is Ethan, we'll be a step closer to ironing all of this out.' She stood as she spoke and tucked her notebook away. 'Will you be okay to leave the details we mentioned with our desk sergeant before you leave?'

'Of course, no trouble at all,' he said, following Melanie to the door. They walked the short journey back to reception in silence.

On arriving back in the entranceway, Melanie turned to again thank their new witness but he cut her off. 'Ethan, he's a good bloke, you know. He likes his women, don't get me wrong, but he isn't a git about it.'

Melanie flashed a tight smile. 'Thank you, Mr Gallagher. We'll be in touch soon, I'm sure.' She exchanged another brief handshake with the man before going back through the double doors leading into the station proper. She pulled her phone out and swiped down to Carter's number; he answered within two rings. 'Are you upstairs?'

'Most of us are, boss. What's up?'

'Get everyone together, would you?' Melanie said, climbing the stairs to meet her team. 'We've got ourselves a victim.'

12

The team were spread out across two cars: Melanie, Carter and Burton in one, while Fairer and Read followed in another. Morris had been excused on account of now having a digital footprint to track down. Melanie had left Morris rifling through everything she could find out about Ethan Irwill, while the rest of the team prepared themselves to start a hunt through the man's private possessions – or, worse still, his murder scene. It was a thought that had crossed Melanie's mind more than once since they'd hit the address into the GPS system, but she hadn't shared it with her juniors. Carter was already far too enthusiastic, and Melanie didn't want to encourage him.

'You're being a real ambulance-chaser about all of this, you know?' Burton's curt tone caught Melanie's attention. She'd been wrapped up in reading through the slim file they'd managed to pull together on Ethan already, but the conversation between her colleagues was growing a little heated.

'Is that a politically correct term to be using?' Carter replied. He was driving, one eye on the GPS and one eye on the road. From his profile Melanie could see that he was smirking.

'I'm just saying, for someone with a kid at home–'

'Oh, Burton, don't bring Emily into this, you're better than that.'

She shrugged. 'I'm just saying.'

Melanie looked over her shoulder to raise an eyebrow at Burton before looking back toward the windscreen. 'You both seem pretty chipper, all things considered.'

'We've got a lead. We should be pleased, right?' Carter replied.

'Hm, maybe.' Melanie looked down at the file again. 'I'd be more nervous about the bloody mess that we might find on the other side of this man's front door, if I were you.'

Melanie authorised the team to make their way indoors, providing their hands were gloved and their feet covered, while she thanked the entry crew that had gained them access.

'Protective gear, in this heat?' Fairer moaned.

'What's the heat got to do with being careful at a crime scene?' Burton snapped. She punctuated her comment by pulling up the zip of her suit, and her colleagues stayed quiet.

Burton was the first to approach the open doorway. When she pushed the door open a little wider on entry, she felt resistance between the wood and the wall behind it. She ducked to retrieve a wad of post that had been pushed out the way, at least four or five days' worth, if she had to guess.

'Check whatever the letter is on the bottom of the pile,' Melanie said, coming to a halt behind Burton. 'That'll give us a starting point for what our timeline might be.' She paused to take in a hard breath from the stale hallway. 'I guess we're not dealing with a murder scene.'

'Carter would have been gagging by now if we were,' she joked. 'Besides, in this heat? We'd smell a body a mile off.'

Burton followed her superior, ripping into the bottom letter – as swiftly as her gloves would allow – as she went along. Although the gloves were a minor irritation compared to the shoe coverings that caused a rustle with every step.

'He's been gone for five or six days if his post is anything to go by,' Burton announced, following Melanie into the living room where Carter and Read were tentatively looking through drawers already.

'No signs at all of a struggle though, so did he go willingly?' Melanie asked the room.

'Jesus!' The exclamation came from somewhere outside of the living area but before any of the team could rush to investigate, Fairer wandered in through an open doorway at the end of the room; presumably leading from the kitchen. 'Based on this, I can confirm it's been five or six days.' With one gloved finger hooked underneath the handle, he held a one-pint milk carton a safe distance away from himself for the team to behold.

'One pint, eh? Sign of the lonely bachelor,' Carter said before turning back to the open drawer in front of him.

'You'd know,' Read snapped with a stutter of laughter that was echoed by Fairer. Carter laughed as well although Burton sensed it was forced.

Leaving the boys to their jokes, Burton stepped back out into the hallway to investigate the room opposite the living space. It looked to be a small home office. There was a desk wedged underneath the front window to give a good view of the garden, and filing cabinets positioned at regular intervals around the room. He'd made a comfortable space for himself, with a small biscuit barrel balanced on the windowsill and, to Burton's surprise, a thick scented candle at the edge of the work desk.

She was drawn to the photographs pinned to the walls behind the desk too: one of Ethan with what Burton thought must be his mother; then another with both of them looking older, his mother's hair had thinned, her skin paled. Burton remembered Melanie having mentioned Ethan's mother passing away. There was no sign of the father in the pictures.

There was a Bachelor of Arts certificate amidst the photographs: digital media, a subject Burton frowned over. She didn't know exactly what it involved, but it sounded more up Morris' street than her own. The degree was tacked lower than the images of Ethan with his mother, as though the frames had been hung in a hierarchy. When she heard the thud of footfalls coming down the stairs, Burton turned back to the doorway in time to see Melanie come to a stop there.

The DI leaned in to take a look around the room. 'Let me guess, no signs of a struggle in here either?' she asked.

Burton shook her head. 'There must be something, because there always is, somewhere. But no, no signs of a struggle. I haven't heard much hollering from the testosterone triplets though, so maybe they've found something to keep themselves amused.'

Melanie let out a curt laugh. 'Do you think they get worse as they get older?'

Burton felt a twinge of sadness; no one would ever ask that of their missing victim.

Melanie closed her eyes to rub a fingertip against each eyelid, and a sigh followed. 'Okay, the only option I can see is that we bag and box as much as we can and get it back to the station to start going through things properly.' She turned and crossed the hall to the remaining members of the team and Burton followed, not in the least bit surprised to catch Read stashing his phone away as they stepped into the room. 'Anything happening in here?' Melanie said.

Carter nodded toward the coffee table. 'We've found other posted items. There's nothing suspicious, more bills mostly, but it might give us an idea of his daily habits, that sort of thing.

Fairer found some interesting printouts under the side table, mind you,' he said, leaning forward to pick up what Burton saw were images of small holiday homes.

'Cottages?' she asked.

'Cottages, lodges, one or two caravan parks.'

'So, he was planning a holiday?' Melanie asked.

'Without telling anyone though?' Carter replied.

'Good point. Bag it along with anything else of interest. Burton has found an office across the way, so we'll get started on packing that up and getting it back to the station in lots.'

'What are we treating this as though?' Carter asked, pulling Melanie back into the room.

She turned to reply but the sound of her phone ringing cut through the space. 'Ah, perfect timing,' she said, spotting the name on the screen. 'Morris, what have you got?'

Melanie stepped outside to take the phone call, leaving Burton and Carter to browse the holiday prints. Carter passed a handful over to his colleague while he continued to flick through one or two others.

'I'm getting a bad feeling about all of this,' he eventually said, staring down at an image of a photo-improved caravan.

'I thought you were excited?'

'All of this though.' He gestured around the room with the paper. 'He's missing but he's not and he's dead, but we don't have a body and – I don't know, it feels off, don't you think?'

Burton smiled. 'Carter, it's felt off since we confiscated a video of a man being stifled. You're just catching up.' She gave her colleague a gentle nudge as Melanie walked back in.

'Right, Morris has found as much as she can without having hands-on access to a laptop, so that's our first port of call when it comes to taking things back. What she has found is that Ethan hasn't withdrawn money from any bank accounts in the last five days, nor has he been active on social media, from what she can see on the outskirts.'

'So where does that leave us?' Carter asked, setting the papers back on the table.

'Bag everything that could be useful. Laptop, holiday brochures, bills. I want everything back at the station before the day is out. By the looks of things, Ethan Irwill is a missing person at best; a murder victim most likely, so evidence-wise we'll take whatever we can get.'

Burton felt a twist in her stomach as she followed her superior outside to grab empty boxes from the cars. It was her job to do this, and she'd work the case as well as she could. But facing off against another murderer so soon wasn't exactly her idea of ideal.

13

The shared office space had become a storage unit for cardboard boxes. Melanie hadn't realised quite how much raw material was being removed from Ethan's home; but the more they had to look through the better their chances were. Carter announced the arrival of the final box as he thumped it down hard on the edge of Morris' desk, pulling her attention from whatever was on her screen. She grimaced as Carter used his forearm to mop sweat from his brow but her look softened when Carter explained, 'Tech equipment.' He tapped the lid.

'Oh.' Morris' face lit up in such a way that Melanie had to smile. 'Come to mama,' the DC said, pulling back cardboard folds to get to the underneath.

'Remember when she was quiet?' Carter said as he joined Melanie at the evidence board.

'I sort of prefer her like this,' she replied. 'At least JOC will know we've got someone serious on the job.'

'When are they arriving?'

'According to the blunt-force voicemail I picked up first thing this morning, any time this afternoon.' She turned to face the blank space behind them. 'We need something on this by the end of the day though, Carter. I'm not going to have hauled this bloke's life in here for nothing.'

'Understood. Fairer and Read are going through stuff we pulled from the living room. Irwill had a whole drawer full of post, all opened and dealt with, but it looks like he was a man who kept things.'

'Thank fuck for that. Maybe we'll stand a chance of finding him.' Melanie knew her tone was sharp, but it had already been a long day for everyone, and they were barely halfway through it. 'What's your plan? Are you with Burton?'

'The state of her,' he said, nodding toward Burton. She was running her hands through her hair, and staring down at ten boxes of paperwork. 'We'll take a box each and hope for the best. I'll give Morris' share of the paperwork to Read and Fairer,' Carter said as he turned to face the general work area. 'It looks like she's set for a while where she is.' Melanie followed Carter's eyeline and spotted Morris squinting into the back panel of Ethan's laptop. Morris flashed an excited expression before setting the machine to one side and writing something down.

Melanie shrugged. 'I still prefer her like this.'

It was some time later when, from the corner of her eye, Melanie noticed the office door swing open to let a newcomer into the shared space. She was a petite woman, in her late fifties if Melanie had to guess, with a stern expression and a briefcase in tow. There were laughter lines stretching out from beneath oversized glasses and she wore a thick jacket, despite the heat. Melanie assumed this was the visit she'd been waiting for. She crossed the space between them and set her face to a smile, prepared to greet the stranger on friendly terms. 'Can I help you?'

'Are you DI Watton?'

'I am.'

'Then yes, you can.'

The woman's expression softened as she extended a hand and Melanie was glad to see the change. 'I'm DS Stretton, Polly from the joint operations cell. I believe you logged a call with us recently about a case you're working on?'

'I did. Could we step into my office for this?'

The team were so rapt in their investigations, they hardly seemed to notice the person they'd all been waiting for had arrived. Inside their privacy, Melanie closed the door and took a deep in-breath before sitting down opposite the visitor, who had already made herself comfortable. Stretton set her briefcase on the floor next to her chair, leaned back, and flashed open hands at Melanie, as though giving her the proverbial floor to speak.

'We think we've got a snuff film,' Melanie announced. There was no easy or soft way of saying it, and Melanie didn't want this meeting to last any longer than it needed to. 'We've found footage of a man being stifled, our medical examiner has authenticated it as best as he can, and we've very recently gained access to what looks to be our victim's home.'

'Evidence from the crime scene?'

'We don't have a crime scene.'

Stretton's eyes stretched wide. 'My, this is a juicy one.'

'It seems to be. Our technology expert, DC Morris–'

'I'm sorry, is that DC Lucy Morris?'

'It is,' Melanie answered. Stretton gestured for her to continue again and Melanie did so, despite the new knot in her stomach. 'DC Morris thought we might benefit from looking into forums on the dark web. I'm afraid she's more equipped to explain these things than I am. I can get her?'

Stretton thought for a moment and said, 'Have you found anything on any of the forums to support the dark web theory?'

'We've found talk of snuff films, yes, but nothing that explicitly explains away the case we're looking into.'

Stretton batted her questions across one after the other and

Melanie tried to answer at the same pace. After a quick twenty minutes, Stretton said, 'And you'd like permission to keep looking into this line of enquiry?'

'Yes, we would.'

'Can I be frank?'

'Please,' Melanie said, her stomach muscles now a cat's cradle.

'We're currently investigating a paedophile ring that stretches from UK soil across most of Europe. That case must be our top priority for the foreseeable future. That's point one. My second point: is DC Morris a permanent member of your team?'

'She is.'

'She has no training days planned?'

Melanie tried to hold back a frown. 'None that I'm aware of, no.'

'I'm familiar with Morris' work. JOC works closely with the technology teams across the country and her name has come up more than once. You're in good hands with her, be sure of that.'

Melanie felt herself unclench, but she knew it couldn't be this easy.

Stretton continued. 'However, I'd like to arrange a training day for her, for dark web investigations specifically. If you can spare her for a day, two at most, I can spare this case and let you keep it. Assuming that's what you want?'

'My team are eager to see this through, yes.'

Stretton collected her briefcase and rose from her seat. 'In that case, DI Watton, it's been a pleasure meeting you.' She extended her hand and Melanie quickly stood and matched the gesture. It seemed the newcomer was eager to leave and get back to her own investigations; although, Melanie couldn't exactly blame her. The DI stepped around the desk and made for the door, but Stretton stopped her in her tracks. 'It's no trouble, I can see myself out.' She smiled before setting her face back to the same neutral expression she'd entered the room with.

'Thanks so much for your time, DS Stretton,' Melanie said to the retreating woman, unsure of whether she'd hear the farewell or not.

Stretton had barely set a foot outside of Melanie's office when Carter stuck his head around the doorway. 'That didn't take you long,' Melanie said.

'That didn't take *you* long. How did it go?'

'We're keeping the case,' Melanie said, dropping back into her chair. 'And Morris has earnt herself a large coffee with a brownie on the side.'

When the team had been filled in on the result of the meeting, they fell back into their workloads. Melanie was looking through Ethan's most recent bank statements. So far there hadn't been anything surprising; he ate takeaways, used a fair amount of petrol, paid his bills on time. There weren't extravagant purchases to suggest a girlfriend, or a blackmailer, although his weekend charges supported Gallagher's story that the boys liked their booze – but Melanie hardly saw that as a reason for murder. The only one anomaly she'd found was a recent payment made through PayPal, and she wrote up a Post-it to remind her to check-in with Morris about it.

'Knock knock,' Carter said from the open doorway.

'News?'

'Sort of.' He came in and sat opposite Melanie. He handed her a stack of papers. 'Burton and I found more holiday home printouts stashed away in the study.'

'So, he was planning a trip for a while? Or he was planning

to buy somewhere? I don't understand why we keep finding these. Theories?'

'We've got Morris checking through Irwill's internet history to see if we can find logic for why he was looking at these places. What she's found so far is this,' he said, lifting up one final sheet. 'It's a document listing all of the locations.' He handed the sheet over and Melanie scanned through the columns: place, price, availability, distance. 'He was keeping some sort of log of these places but we can't work out why.'

'The distance column: is there anything to support this in his internet history? Was he driving to these places?'

'No, but he might have been planning to,' Morris said as she walked into the office. 'For every property, we've got a route planner. That's where the distance comes from.'

'Do you think one of these properties is the place on the tape?' Carter asked.

Melanie scanned the sheets. It suddenly felt like she had up to ten murder scenes on her desk, with no way of knowing where to start. 'There's nothing on that computer to indicate which one of these he went for?'

Morris shook her head. 'I'll keep looking, but I haven't found anything so far.'

'There's a transaction on this bank statement, something to do with PayPal,' Melanie said, highlighting the entry in yellow. She handed the sheet to Morris. 'Can you track this down?'

'I'll bump it to the top of the pile.'

'Until then we're going to have to think about checking out as many of these spots as we can.' Melanie looked down the column of properties. 'You take the top half and I'll take the bottom? We'll try to contact the owners to see whether the properties have been used recently.'

'I've got a better idea.' Burton burst in. She held up a folder like a sporting trophy. 'Ethan has a printed copy of email exchanges between him and, I'd guess from context, the owner of one of those properties.' Burton pointed to the paper that Carter was clutching before handing her own file to Melanie. 'He printed everything, or someone printed it and gave it to him, either way–'

'We've got something,' Melanie finished.

'We've got more than something,' Burton said, her tone smug. 'In that file, there was a lease agreement.'

14

With Burton behind the wheel, Melanie stared down at the papers in front of her. From the back seat Carter navigated from the map on his phone, instructing Burton when to turn and which way. He gave his colleague ample warning to negotiate tight corners, considering the faster-than-advised speed she was driving at. Read and Fairer had stayed behind at the office to fully document the evidence the team had spent the morning going through. Meanwhile, Melanie had pulled in a car of uniformed officers that were driving close behind, to give her the security of more living bodies on the ground should they be needed. She was studying the victim's papers for their destination; each alternative route was highlighted in a different colour, the journey times scribbled alongside them. She couldn't make sense of this.

'Next two lefts, Chris, and then we're about five minutes away,' Carter announced, pulling himself forward to pop his head through the space between the front seats. 'What are we expecting to find here, boss?'

Melanie dropped the papers. 'I mean, does anyone ever want to find a body?'

'Better than not knowing where he is still,' Burton replied.

'Jesus, what an alternative.' Carter dropped himself against the back seat.

'I have no idea what we're expecting, Edd. I'm hoping for something, whatever it is.'

'Next right, Burton.'

She rounded the corner and no sooner had the road straightened out in front of them, there appeared a sign for the holiday cottages. Between the blue sky and the brilliant green of the overhanging trees, the entrance looked like something stripped straight from a brochure.

'Follow that sign,' Carter said, leaning forward again. 'Okay, we're straight for another half a mile or so and then according to this we should come to more of a path than a road, and the cottages are dotted along that strip.'

'So, we're keeping our eyes out for lucky number fifteen,' Melanie said, staring out the window as she spoke. There were seventeen cottages listed along the path, so they already knew that Ethan's must be somewhere toward the end. *As out of the way as he could have booked*, Melanie thought. 'Comfortable going any faster than this?' She knew that her tone was cutting but there wasn't a polite way of asking the question. From the blank expression on Burton's face as she pressed her foot down harder against the accelerator, Melanie didn't think the other officer felt especially offended.

The ground of the off-road crunched under the wheels as Burton hit it with speed, driving straight past one, two, three cottages. She wore a determined expression while her colleagues wore frantic ones; Melanie and Carter were both staring from their windows like eager birdwatchers. *If only there would be a weekend away at the end of this journey*, Melanie thought. Several more cottages flew past the windows as Burton pressed on, coming to an abrupt halt when an unexpected fork in the road appeared. Carter fumbled with his phone for further guidance. Before Melanie could hurry him along, Burton made her own choice and steered the car left. Melanie eyed her junior's profile, her stern-set expression.

'What?' Burton said, as though sensing her superior's stare. 'He can't get more dead, can he? We'll just come back on ourselves.'

'Jesus, Chris,' Carter said, echoing Melanie's own surprise.

Burton kept her eyes ahead and let out a soft sigh. She didn't speak again until she jerked the car forward with a hard slam on the brakes. 'Fifteen,' she announced, looking through the wind-screen toward a quiet and picturesque cottage with a backdrop of woodland, complete with rich trees casting shadows on the ground. Twenty feet in front of the doorway there was a small wooden sign confirming the number of the property.

'Nicely done,' Melanie said, popping open her seat belt. Carter and Burton followed, exiting the vehicle along with their superior as the patrol car came to a stop behind them. The two teams gathered in front of the property. 'We're going to scout the perimeter, but the likely course of action is that we're going to have to force entry. Everyone okay to cover the surrounding areas?' Melanie spoke to the group, but it was the driver of the patrol team who nodded his understanding on their behalf.

They set about distributing themselves around the small building. The uniformed officers, their foreheads already shining with sweat, formed a square at four points around the property while Carter and Burton stepped either side. Melanie cupped out the interrupting sun to shield her vision as she leaned toward the right-hand window at the front of the space. Inside she could see a small kitchen that was neat, white and didn't look like it had been trashed or left in a hurry. She stepped to the other window then, keeping an ear out for her officers as she moved. *No luck for them either*, she thought. She repeated the same hand gesture from before to shield her vision. The second window only showed what looked to be a hallway, and a small inside porch where there was a pair of shoes and two coats.

'Burton, Carter,' she hollered. When they appeared from their respective sides, she said, 'We're going in. We're not going to find what we need from outside.'

Carter turned in the direction of the car, to fetch the entryway kit, Melanie assumed, but sometimes a good twist would do the trick...

'Carter.' When he turned, Melanie was clutching the handle to a partially open door. *It was good to have easy entry*, she thought, *but that hadn't even been locked*. 'We won't need the kit but be ready, okay?' She looked from Carter to Burton, and then back toward the cottage. 'We have no idea what we're walking into.'

Melanie pushed the door back gently, causing a theatrical creak. The property remained silent, so she stepped forward into the space with her two colleagues close behind. In a natural formation, the three officers split in their separate directions as though the search was rehearsed. Burton stepped into what Melanie had already seen was the kitchen while Carter started to climb the stairs, pausing between each tread. Melanie went deeper into the property, following the small hallway towards a closed door – but a wooden barrier couldn't shield the smell entirely.

Melanie placed a hand underneath her nose as she pressed the door open, unleashing a mess of smells that spread around the space at speed. She recognised the blend of eggs, cabbage; dead skin that had been left alone for too long. As the smell spread through the house it must have reached Burton, who quickly appeared with a thumb and forefinger piercing her nostrils closed.

'Boss, that smells like–'

'Oh arses, is that decomp?' Carter cut in as he thumped down the stairs.

'It certainly smells like it, kids,' Melanie said, holding her nose a pinch tighter. 'Let's get this over with.' She walked through and took a quick glance about her, recognising without a doubt the room they'd seen in the video footage. It only took another four or five steps around a jutting wall, positioned to separate out the room, and there it was: the decomposing body of Ethan Irwill.

Melanie put out an arm to prevent her officers walking further into the crime scene. 'Don't, we don't have any of the gear we need.' She turned to face them. 'Irwill isn't going anywhere. We need to back-step out the way we came.'

Once her and her colleagues had refuelled their lungs with outside air, Melanie felt better equipped to deliver her instructions. 'Burton, fill in the uniforms and tell them we'll need them to set up a cordon. Carter, can you call this in with Read and Fairer? You'll need to call forensics after that and let them know what we've found. Tell them it's hot, would you? Really bloody hot in there.' Melanie rubbed a hand across her forehead, appreciating for the first time the sweated reaction that was half heat and half the shock of what they'd found.

'Are you heading up to the site owners?' Carter said, his phone already in his hand. 'One of us will need to let them know what's happening.'

'I'll head up there after,' Melanie replied. 'First, we need George Waller out here.'

15

George Waller pushed his way through the group of police officers who were huddled around the entrance to the cottage. With little grace, he ripped his gloves from his hands and pulled away the mask that had seconds ago covered his mouth and nose. The medical examiner threw his head back in a dramatic gesture, and with a noise that resembled a heave he pulled in a great mouthful of air, expelling hard into Melanie's face as she came to greet him.

'Christ, I love the smell of decomposition in the afternoon,' he said, pulling down the zip that held together his protective suit. As the fabric split open down his torso, George made a show of sniffing in the general direction of his clothing, and then more specifically at his underarms. 'And twenty-six degree heat; let's not forget the twenty-six degree heat.'

'Are you finished?' Melanie said.

George unzipped the rest of his plastic sheath and shrugged it off to the floor. 'Yes, yes I think I am.' He collected up the mess of protective coverings that lay around him. 'Obviously I can't do a formal identification, but I'd say he's the man you're looking for. Based on the bloating and the bleeding and the...' he trailed off and inhaled hard again. 'The God-awful stench, of course. I'd say that he's been here for anywhere between three and five days. When I get him back to the lab I should be able to tell you more, but we'll have to factor in heat conditions, which will have had a hand in the state of things.'

Melanie ran a hand through her hair. 'How's your table looking?'

'Free enough. I can start on him first thing in the morning.'

'Not this afternoon?'

George looked down at his watch. 'No, detective, not this afternoon. The only help I've got is on sick leave, and don't think I can't see the joke there.'

Melanie knew not to force the issue. 'Okay, if you need help moving him then wrangle a uniform or two for the heavy lifting.' She left George to his work and stepped toward the forensics team who were unfolding from a black Range Rover. The only colleague of the bunch who she recognised was Graham Williams; the forensics officer who was on the case when their second body appeared last year. The two greeted each other with a slim smile. 'Long time no see,' Melanie said.

The sentiment encouraged a soft grin from Graham. 'If only the circumstances were better.'

'If only.' Melanie turned to face the cottage and Graham joined her. 'Dead body, warm cottage, definite murder.'

'Something suspicious about the body?' Graham asked.

'Not quite. The suspicious thing was having a video of the murder circulated around the local area days before we'd even found the body.' Melanie saw Graham's glance shift from the property to her and back again. 'I know.'

'Medical examiner here?'

'He's readying to remove our man from inside. We'll need the rest of the house–'

'Melanie,' Graham interrupted her, 'it's not our first rodeo at a crime scene.'

Melanie turned to face her colleague and he matched the manoeuvre. 'We've got a strong cordon set up here so you shouldn't be interrupted, and we can secure access to the cottage for as long as necessary. One of my team is tracking down the property owner as we speak. Keep me up to speed?'

'Of course.' He gestured one of his team over towards him. 'But from what you've said, we'll be here for a while.'

Morris had just set down her black marker pen, having finished writing on the evidence board, when the main door to the office rushed open. Melanie walked in, followed by Carter and Burton, and Melanie immediately clocked Morris standing by the board.

'You've got something?' Melanie said, crossing the room.

'I've got plenty.'

'Hit us.'

'First of all, Ethan has a disturbingly organised desktop. Everything is filed away under appropriate headings and some items even had times and dates in the headings–'

'Is being organised that weird?' Carter interrupted.

'Have you seen your desktop lately?' Burton said, and Carter flashed a fair-enough expression. 'Sorry, Morris, don't mind us.'

'Second of all,' Morris continued, 'Ethan has a colourful internet history both in terms of his pornographic viewings and in terms of his research interests. The porn is mostly torture and submissive stuff but, honestly, I'm not prepared to watch it for long enough to know more than that. Maybe Carter will.'

Carter placed a hand theatrically on his chest. 'I'm shocked; shocked and offended.'

The light-hearted interval allowed everyone a breath before

Morris addressed her other discoveries. 'That said, Ethan has done *a lot* of research into snuff films, including compiling lists of ones that he's managed to track down and ones that he can't find. I've done a search on the laptop and I've found a couple of digital versions of some, but it might be worth looking out for DVDs or unmarked discs in his belongings. He also has a separate document where he ranks their believability.'

'I don't get it,' Burton said, jumping in while Morris paused for breath. 'None of the snuff films that he's watched are actually real snuff films, is that right?'

'There allegedly are no snuff films,' Melanie answered. 'They're an urban myth.'

'Except for Ethan's own.' Morris pulled back the attention of her colleagues. 'And, if that weren't enough, there's also dark web software on Ethan's computer but it's password protected. I'm currently using a scrambler to decipher what the password is but that could take a little while to work out the right code. The same applies for the encrypted files I've found.'

'Is there any way to know how long the password-thingy will take?'

'Wait, what encrypted files?'

Morris answered Melanie's question first. 'I knew you'd pick up on that, boss. There is a folder on Ethan's laptop that I can't open. I found it tucked out of the way in a folder marked "personal interests" which, incidentally, is where I found all of his snuff research so I'm assuming that whatever is in this file has something to do with the film, or his research before the film. But until I can unencrypt the file, there's no way of accessing the contents.'

'And the password-thingy?' Carter asked again.

'I should have access to his dark web software before lunchtime tomorrow, depending on how advanced his protection is. The scrambler won't work for an encrypted file though.'

'What will?' Melanie said.

Morris sighed. 'I've tried the usual programmes that I'd use for something like this but, truthfully, it's kind of trial and error for me right now. I'm wary of compromising the contents of the file but I also want to try as many options as I can before taking it to the tech team.'

'Don't be proud, Morris, just take it to them,' Carter said.

'They'll run the same programmes as I can run here so I may as well rule them out before I bother them with anything.'

'You're doing the right thing, Morris. Ignore Carter, he's just got a lot of opinions this week,' Melanie said, throwing Carter a playful smile. 'This is great, really good work. Do we have any work records, anything we can work with in terms of tracing his habits?'

Morris reached to the table next to her to pick up a small pile of paper. 'I've made printouts of everything in his work folder, including details of the last company he was working with. Everything looks like contractor or freelancer work, but there's still a paper trail to follow.'

'Brilliant.' Melanie took the paperwork from Morris and handed it over to Burton. 'You and Carter can get started on this. Morris, you'll keep working on the laptop?'

'My pleasure,' Morris said, and Melanie sensed she really meant it. 'But there's another thing,' she added as Melanie started to turn away. Melanie was optimistic for another reveal but from Morris' expression she sensed there wasn't one coming. 'DS Stretton from JOC has contacted me about the training session.'

Melanie sighed hard. 'When?'

'This weekend.'

'Shit.' Melanie rubbed at her temples. 'It's not ideal timing but fair is fair. You'll miss out on the overtime schedule.' Melanie smiled to try to soften her first reaction.

'But think of all the fun I'm going to have,' Morris replied, matching the lighter tone.

'Right then, let's get cracking, folks. I'll see what Read and Fairer have brought in.' Melanie watched as the detectives distributed themselves around the office. Morris powered back to her own desk while Carter and Burton shared the paperwork out between them on the way to theirs. Whatever Read and Fairer were doing, they were hunched over phones and computer screens and, for once, they looked genuinely busy with their work. Melanie let out another hard sigh and ran a hand through her hair. 'What to do, what to do...' she trailed off, her thoughts distracted by the sound of her mobile ringing from her front pocket. Melanie pulled the handset out to a familiar name on the screen: George Waller.

16

Read and Fairer perched on the edge of a well-worn two-seater sofa on the far side of the room they'd been guided into. The owner of the holiday cottage turned crime scene, a Mr Unwin, wasn't at all what Read had expected. A sweet-seeming chap in his late sixties if Read had to guess. Mr Unwin had seen both officers in and told them to make themselves comfortable and, despite their protests, had then disappeared to make tea. In the distance, Read could hear the clatter of cutlery against crockery as spoons hit cups and a kettle started to steam.

'He could have been in on this, you know?' Fairer cut through the silence of the room.

Read turned to face his partner. 'Are you serious?'

'Why wouldn't I be?'

'Brian, come on, look at the bloke.'

'He owns the crime scene.'

'It's a bloody holiday let.'

'I'm just saying.' Fairer edged forward in his seat to get a better look at his colleague. 'The rest of this sodding case hardly makes any sense, does it? Why are you assuming he isn't involved when–'

'Gentleman.' Mr Unwin appeared in the doorway. He held a tray with three mugs and a teapot balanced on top of it. 'I hope you don't mind it from the pot. So few people seem to do it these days.' He set the tray down and took a seat in the opposing armchair, gesturing for the officers to pour their own drinks.

Read inched forward to reach for the tray. 'Thank you, Mr Unwin. If you don't mind, we were hoping to ask you a few questions about your property? The holiday lease that we called about?' Read glanced up in time to catch the older gentleman signal his consent. 'The man that you rented it to.'

'Ethan Irwill, was it?' Fairer clarified.

Unwin shook his head lightly. 'A crying shame, isn't it? Who'd want to do such a thing?'

'Did you ever meet Mr Irwill to arrange anything with the booking?' Fairer continued.

'I didn't, no. My daughter, she tries to get me to do this internet business and it's too complicated for me. I had a number listed and he called to say he was interested in renting the property from me for a while.'

'How long is a while?' Read asked, sitting back with his tea.

Unwin's forehead furrowed. 'Ten days, if memory serves right.'

'He was there the entire ten nights?'

'That I can't tell you, officer. The keys stay at the reception for the site, you see. He told me they'd be going up to collect them on the day the lease started, but whether they did or not...' He shrugged. 'You could ask at the reception though. They're meant to have a log of the keys coming in and out. Mind you, I never know–'

'Mr Unwin, I'm sorry,' Fairer interrupted. '*They* would be going to collect the keys; you're sure Mr Irwill said they?'

'Yes, he said, "We'll be coming to collect the keys," I'm sure that's what he...' Mr Unwin trailed off. 'Is that important?'

'Did you have two names for the booking?' Read asked.

'No, it was just Mr Irwill on paper, although there was a second email contact listed without a name. It's a two-person place, three at a push, so I didn't mind that there would be more people there, as long as they were treating the place right. Is that important?' he repeated, sitting forward in his seat this time.

'It may well be,' Read said, trying to use a soft tone.

'And how did Mr Irwill pay for the rental, Mr Unwin, was that in cash?' Fairer picked up.

'No, no. That did go through on the internet. That Pay what's-it.'

'PayPal?'

'That's the one.'

Read made a note of this. He had a half-memory of Melanie mentioning a PayPal transaction on Irwill's bank statements.

The two officers continued for a further five minutes before coming to a natural pause in their questions. It was clear that Mr Unwin didn't know anything more than he'd said already.

'There's nothing else I can help you with?' the man asked as the officers stepped closer to the front door.

'You've been a great help already, thank you. We'll be in touch if there's anything else,' Read said. 'And the station will be in touch when we've finished with the property. Any questions about that, you can call my colleague here, okay, Mr Unwin? Brian Fairer, right there on the card,' Read said, pressing a card into the man's hand as he stepped out of the open doorway.

On the trek back towards the car Read and Fairer walked level with each other.

'Did you genuinely give that man my card?'

'Why, nervous that the old murderer is going to call you?' Read replied, his tone much lighter than that of his colleague.

As the two men climbed in opposite sides of their shared vehicle Fairer looked over the top to catch Read's eye. 'You're a real tosser sometimes, and if that old codger kills me, you're going to feel really bad about it.'

Superintendent Beverly Archer gestured for Melanie to take a seat. The senior officer was mid-conversation, taking down notes at a terrifying speed. Melanie remained still and quiet while her boss continued, as she surveyed the room for something to do. There were still no signs of a family; still no signs of a world outside of this space. But the phone colliding into its cradle on the desk grabbed Melanie's attention back. Archer continued writing for a second or two longer before letting out a hard breath, setting down her pen, and locking eyes with Melanie.

'Don't sugar-coat it, Mel, tell me what we know.'

Melanie sat upright in the chair; her spine braced for impact. 'Waller is readying himself for the autopsy. He called to ask for a copy of the footage, so he can try to match what we see on the tape to the injuries on the body. Read and Fairer have a meeting with the property owner for the cottage where we found the body, to try to establish who it was rented to, how they communicated and the rest of it.' Melanie paused, having noticed that her superior was making patchy notes on a scrap sheet of paper. She waited until Archer had caught up. 'Burton and Carter are going in to see the victim's employer, or his most recent employer at least, they should be talking by now. We're hoping it'll give us a clearer idea of who he was, what he was up to.'

'Morris?' Arched pushed, having caught up with her notes.

'Morris is ripping apart the victim's laptop. She's found several things of use already but there is a lot of encrypted information there that she's trying to get access to. She'll also be out of bounds to us for the weekend because JOC are scooping her up for a training session.'

'In terms of the laptop, are the tech team of no use to her?' Archer queried with a cutting tone, but Melanie tried not to let it throw her off.

'She knows the early procedures for it. Morris thought, and I agreed, that her time would be best spent going through the things that she knows for certain they'll try, and then when and if she does take the equipment to them, these preliminary tests will have been completed. We should have some answers before she goes away, at least.'

Archer nodded; her lips thinned. 'And what are you doing?'

'I'll shortly be contacting Fin Gallagher, who was the friend to identify the man from the footage in the first instance. I'm hoping he can give us more names worth contacting and we can set up interviews with the victim's friends. This way we'll get a picture of who Irwill spent his time with, how he spent his time.'

'It sounds like you've got everything in hand,' Archer said, pausing to grab the sheet of paper she'd been writing on when Melanie had first arrived. 'Perhaps you can explain this to me.'

Melanie eyed the sheet as it landed in front of her: Video footage. Dark web. Male victim. Freelancer? Loner? Snuff.

The words jumped out at Melanie in a nonsensical order. 'I don't understand,' she admitted, leaning back from the desk.

'The press know, Mel,' Archer explained. 'I don't know how far-spread this video is. I don't know whether a stupid kid leaked the video, whether a stupid PC shared what they knew, I don't even know whether...'

Archer trailed off and suddenly Melanie could fill in the blank for herself. 'You think there's a leak?'

17

Melanie tucked herself away in her office. She needed the quiet, the time to think. From this viewpoint she could see her team seated at their desks, intermittently throwing information across the room to each other. Archer had received the details from a local newspaper; she'd been on good terms with the editor, who called with the news of a leak before anything had officially been put in to print. 'They'll run something eventually,' Archer said. 'Professional courtesy only goes so far in this business. Plus, all things considered, I suppose we're lucky there hasn't been a leak somewhere sooner.'

But the editor, despite not wanting to reveal full details of the person he'd spoken to, did tell Archer the information came from a woman. Melanie had resisted the accusation – 'If there's a leak then it's spouting from somewhere else.' – but her eyes moved from Morris to Burton and back again, wondering.

Melanie watched as Carter approached her door and knocked gently.

'Come in.'

Carter pushed the door closed behind him after he'd entered. 'Time for a chat?'

'Always. Pull up a pew,' Melanie said, gesturing to the seat opposite her.

'Burton and I went to Ethan's place of work today. It's a media firm based on the other side of town: Silver Linings. It's a web design company primarily, nothing special by the looks of things. Ethan was contracted there on a freelance basis to put together some trailers for their work. The bloke we spoke to, Taylor Dean, he said it's normally the sort of work they'd do themselves; Ethan was only brought in because of how busy they are at the moment.'

'So, where did they find Ethan? Does anyone at the firm know him?'

'Word of mouth.' Carter licked the tip of his finger to part one sheet of paper from another before setting a printed list down in front of Melanie. 'Chris has had a good look through Ethan's records, and it seems as though this is what he does. That's a list of all of the firms he's freelanced with or been a contractor at. She patched it together from the office boxes and a few bits that Morris has found.'

'This is good work.' Melanie felt a twist in her gut at the sound of her DCs' names though. *It couldn't be them*, she reminded herself, *it just couldn't.* She could feel Carter's eyes on her, waiting for a response or an order on how best to proceed, but Melanie couldn't muster anything. She decided the only thing she could do was to share the load of this latest revelation in the case, and hope her DS would have something, anything, to suggest.

'Carter, I need to tell you something and it needs to be completely confidential.' He opened his mouth as though to defend himself from the suggestion, but Melanie spoke over him. 'You don't share this with Burton, is what I mean.' Melanie knew it was an ask, to expect Carter to keep an accusation like this from his partner, but she needed to contain this as best as she could. 'Archer has had a call from the editor of *The Star*. Someone has told them who Ethan is, who he really is. They know Ethan has connections to the dark web, and it looks as though they know this is a real snuff film we've found.'

Carter dropped back in his chair. 'But how?' Melanie locked eyes with him and watched as the realisation hit. Carter's eyes narrowed and his hand reached to his forehead, his fingertips kneading against the skin. 'Bollocks. No – not in this team.'

Carter paced back and forth across the front space of Melanie's office, one palm pressed flat against his forehead as though enough pressure would force an idea out. He snapped his fingers. 'What if it was the killer?'

'What?'

'What if the killer called the newspaper? We already know it's a woman, we've seen her on the video, so what if it was the killer who called the paper, to blow the story open?' Carter sat down opposite his boss as he spoke. This was the closest thing to a reasonable idea he'd had in the last half an hour and he felt determined to make his case.

'Why though?'

'Maybe she wants people to know what she did?' Carter suggested.

Melanie let out a gentle sigh. 'People already know, Carter, she made a fucking recording of the whole thing.'

Carter's eyes widened at Melanie's tone; he couldn't remember the last time he'd heard that kind of snap from her. 'I'm sorry,' she added. 'I don't want it to be Morris or Burton either, but who else knows as much as them?'

'The killer.' Carter's tone was flat. He felt a tug of irritation in his gut that his boss was so quick to believe this of his colleagues. 'Look, if we have reasonable grounds to suspect this might be something to do with the actual case, and not something to do with our team, can we put pressure on the editor?'

'What do you mean by pressure?'

'I mean can we go and talk to him, ask whether the woman was an officer? Did he even see formal identification?' Carter edged forward, his excitement simmering again at the thought of an explanation, maybe even a lead.

'Whoever she is, she showed him evidence enough for him to call Archer and say there's a leak.' Carter sank back at the sound of Melanie's counterpoint. 'He must be pretty convinced that it was a police officer who he spoke to, Edd.' Melanie stood up from her desk and crossed the room to stare out of the front-facing windows that looked onto the main office. Through the partially closed blinds the desk spaces were visible. 'What have you left Burton working on?'

Carter turned to face his boss. 'She's updating the work records that we've got for Ethan in the evidence file. I'm meant to be taking the next jobs back out there to her, but, you know, we got kind of sidetracked and all.'

Returning to her seat, Melanie riffled through sheets of paperwork that were patchworked across her desk before settling on one in particular. 'Give Burton this.' She handed it over. 'They're Fin Gallagher's contact details. I want him in tomorrow for a formal interview. Tell Burton to check my calendar, book him, and chase the names and numbers he left the first time around.'

'Okay, and what am I doing?'

'You're going to *The Star*. If you're so bloody convinced, Carter, then I'm giving you a shot, one shot, you understand, to talk to the editor. If it gets back to Archer then you're on your own with it. Have we got a deal?'

Carter stretched a hand out to shake on the agreement but a

curt knock stopped Melanie from reciprocating. 'For Christ sake,' she muttered. 'Come on.'

Burton pushed the office door open and smiled a quick greeting to her superiors. Carter couldn't believe she was capable of leaking information, especially not now she was right in front of him.

'I'm sorry, boss, George Waller's been on the phone,' Burton said, stepping further into the office as Melanie's concentration slipped. Carter eyed his boss as she turned to search for something in her suit jacket. 'He said he'd been calling your mobile but he couldn't get through.'

Melanie brought the handset into view. 'Shit. There's news?'

'He said he's finished with the autopsy,' Burton replied. 'He's ready when you are.'

18

Melanie hovered outside Waller's examination room for just over ten minutes. With everything else that had happened that week, she wasn't sure she could stand the sight of a corpse on top of it all. But the alternative was going back to the station to face either Burton or Morris – or both – and she wasn't sure she felt up to that either. At least Morris would be leaving soon, although Melanie felt guilty for her relief over that. She straightened herself up and pulled the front of her jacket together before she pushed open the swing door and stepped into the clinic space. She inhaled the sharp scent of cleaning products, a medley of disinfectants and, if she tried hard enough, the bitterness of blood. Melanie took a scan of the room and spotted George, suited in his overalls but sitting at his desk, clicking his mouse at regular intervals.

'I thought you were never going to come in,' he said, staring at the monitor.

'I'm not in the mood for a dead body,' Melanie admitted.

George rushed out a sharp laugh. 'Then you're in the wrong business, detective.' When Melanie didn't reply, George turned to face her. 'You're not going to bite back?'

'Not today, George.'

'Christ.' He stood from his desk and stepped down onto the level floor from his raised corner space. 'Things must be bad over at the Walton Ranch. Want to talk about it?' He walked as he spoke, and Melanie followed. Despite her early apprehensions, she was grateful when they stopped level with a stretch of metal table that held the stitched remains of Ethan Irwill; at least the body had stopped George from talking.

'Maybe we can focus on this problem first?' Melanie nodded towards the cadaver.

'But of course.' George snapped on a glove. 'This is more my expertise anyway.'

Now that he'd been cleaned up, Ethan Irwill looked even younger, sharper, more the attractive professional than he'd seemed when they first found him. Ten years ago, Melanie's friends would have gone wild for Ethan's type on a night out. She could see the lady's man that Fin Gallagher had described; Ethan had been handsome enough for it. But neither his looks nor his personal effects had shown Melanie anything worth dying for.

She watched as different parts of his bluish skin lit up beneath Waller's overhead lighting. Once each spotlight was positioned to the examiner's liking, the formalities could properly start.

'You'll see these findings in my official report. There's a digital copy on my computer ready to send but I've got a hard copy if you want something to take home with you.' Melanie noted the assumption that she'd be finishing work, or at least heading home for the day, when this procedure was over. With how busy her mind was, it seemed unlikely. 'If we start here and here.' Waller pointed out bruising that had spread around Ethan's face. 'Consistent with a rough grab and hard application of pressure.'

'Pressure like someone blocking his airways?'

'Why, yes. I can't match it move for move, but the injuries to his face and neck are certainly consistent with the recording. In further support of that,' Waller said, taking a step to his left. He lifted Ethan's left wrist as though he were cradling a small bird and brought it closer to the overhead lights. 'There are markings around both wrists that would imply he was tied up at some point. From the angle of his shoulders on the video it's pretty clear that he was tied, but I can't match it injury for injury without having details of the binds that were used.'

Melanie opened her mouth to speak but Waller beat her to it.

'I know, the binds are with forensics, etcetera and so forth. In the interest of making life easier further down the line, I've measured the width of each ligature mark. Assuming that forensics are finished with their analyses before you've caught the killer, you'll at least be able to match another part of this man's injuries to those that you can see inflicted in the recording.'

Melanie beamed. 'You've thought of everything.'

'Not everything. I've done what I can here in terms of analysing bloods, but the state of decomposition is complicating things. I've had to outsource it, and it could be anything up to a week before we get results back from that. But I think the results are worth waiting for.' Waller looked smug with this closing remark, and Melanie felt as though she was meant to goad him for further information. When the prompt didn't come, the ME rolled his eyes and shook his head like a disappointed child. 'Fine, I'll just tell you. Take a look at this.' He pointed toward the right side of Ethan's neck – the side closest to Melanie. When Waller gently kneaded at the area in question, a small hole grew out of the taut skin.

'Entry wound?' Melanie asked.

'Bingo. It's clear that on the tape he's drinking something, some kind of sedative maybe, but he was definitely injected with something before that as well. Like I said, we won't know what until we get a better breakdown of the bloods, but I'd guess it was an initial sedative. To loosen him up, as it were.'

'Alright, George, you did good,' Melanie admitted, and Waller dipped to bow to the compliment.

'Yes, yes I did.'

'So you're what, relatively confident this is the man from the recording?'

Waller reached down to collect the modesty sheet that was gathered at the foot of the body. In a swift motion he pulled it right up until it covered everything bar the top few inches of the dead man's head. He wheeled the table to the corner of the open space before hitting an entry button on the wall. There was a loud clunk as a door unlocked, revealing the freezer space hidden behind the main operating room. Waller disappeared in there with the body and re-emerged alone. 'Shall we?'

Melanie made her way back toward Waller's desk space at the head of the room. He walked up from behind her and positioned himself next to a bin, so he could remove gloves, mask, overalls and deposit them straight into the clinical waste area. As Waller turned to squeeze hand sanitiser from the container fixed to the wall, he picked up their conversation.

'I can't say this is your Ethan, but I can say near as dammit without doubt that it's the man from the recording. I've said as much in my report as well.' He stepped up onto the raised office space and started to feel around his desk. When his hand came upon a brown cardboard folder Waller quickly checked the contents, and then handed it to Melanie.

'So, all we need now is a formal ID,' Melanie said, taking the documents. 'I'll put you in touch with Gallagher. He's the bloke who identified Ethan from the still that we distributed. I'm meant to be meeting with him tomorrow and – are you listening?'

Waller's head snapped up. 'I was looking for something.' He held up a dull yellow Post-it note with something scribbled across it. 'Fin Gallagher. After my frantic phone call with Burton earlier today she gave me these details, said they'd be useful.'

'Well I hope I get to him before you do,' Melanie said, her tone playful.

'You and me both. I don't want to be sending a distraught man your way. No family to speak of then?' Waller leaned forward and conjured a handful of clicks from his computer before standing; Melanie could tell he wasn't interested in an answer. 'That's me done for the day, detective, unless there's anything else?'

Melanie shook her head. 'Nothing that I can think of.'

'Marvellous.' The ME grabbed the coat that was hanging over the back of his chair and draped it around his shoulders. He collected one or two folders under Melanie's watchful eye and then, seeing to it that everything was stashed into his slim briefcase, he stepped off the raised area and stood level with the DI again. 'It's gone six, so I think that's a fine time to shut up shop for the day.'

Melanie flashed a thin smile. She still wasn't sure this workday was quite finished.

'Can I speak out of turn?' Waller asked.

'Don't you always?'

They shared a friendly look as Waller set a hand lightly on Melanie's shoulder. 'It *is* a fine time to shut up shop for the day, Mel, and you look like shit.' He gave her a gentle squeeze before stepping out of her eyeline and walking toward the double doorway exit of the room.

Melanie blinked hard once, twice, to try to shake away the shock of the remark. 'Thanks, George,' she eventually managed. 'That's just the kind of support I needed.'

19

Carter checked the time on the kitchen clock. He'd have to wake Emily up in half an hour; thanks to an impromptu sleepover orchestrated by Trish the night before. He'd barely made it through the front door when Trish was knocking for it to be opened again. There she stood, brandishing their beautiful child like a lethal weapon.

'I need you to have Emily tonight.'

'We're having a sleepover, Dad!'

If it weren't for the presence of their daughter, this would have been another argument.

'I have a work thing,' Trish said with a tight smile.

Carter crouched level with Emily. 'Are you tall enough to get to the ice cream drawer these days?' Emily's eyes stretched wide. 'Go on, see what flavours we've got.' He watched as his daughter shuffled by him and rushed along the hallway before he turned back to his ex-wife. 'A work thing, that's what you're calling him now?'

'Edd, it's none of your business who I'm–'

'You're right, it isn't. But it is my business when you organise a sleepover at my house on one of your nights without asking me first. I have a breakfast meeting tomorrow, but I guess I'll be having that here now, won't I?'

Trish opened her mouth to respond but Carter stopped her. 'You don't care, I got that. Can you pick her up from school tomorrow or do you have a "work thing" then as well?'

'I'll be there to pick her up from school, like every day.' The reply was said with more spite than Carter thought it warranted.

The two said their goodbyes and Carter's quiet evening gave way to ice cream and another run-through of the live-action Cinderella. When he'd called Melanie to re-arrange their meeting spot for the next morning, she'd said she didn't mind at all. But Carter wasn't sure how he felt about bringing murder to the breakfast table.

There was a light tap against the front door the following morning. Outside, Melanie was waiting with two large coffees wedged into a carrier, accompanied by a much smaller cup.

'Coffee?' Melanie said, stepping over the threshold. 'Emily drinks espresso, right?'

Carter faltered. 'That's a nice thought but–'

'Edd.' Her face cracked into a grin. 'I'm not a complete novice. It's hot chocolate.' She stepped through into Carter's kitchen as though she'd been in the house a thousand times, and Carter felt thrown by the familiarity.

'Take a seat,' Carter said, motioning to the breakfast bar. 'Ready for this?'

Melanie popped the plastic lid from her drink and took a large gulp. 'Hit me.'

'Five foot eight, maybe even five nine; brown hair but it could have been a wig, her eyebrows looked a much lighter shade; a northern accent, which sounded authentic although softened, maybe from years spent out of her original area,' he read from a sheet in front of him. 'Sound like anyone we know?'

Melanie thought for a second. 'No, I don't think so. Should it?'

'Archer's editor friend wouldn't give up much, but this is the description he gave of the woman who he met with about the snuff case.'

'Did she have a warrant card?'

Carter flashed a smirk. 'As it turns out, no.'

'But he told Archer–'

'The woman told him that she was off duty, so she wasn't carrying a warrant card, but she knew enough about the case to convince him – his words. Apparently, he forgot to mention that part to Archer when he called for her reaction.'

Melanie shut her eyes as the in-between details dawned on her. 'He called Archer on a fishing expedition.'

'Seems that way.'

Melanie reached across the counter to grab the description and then looked past Carter. 'Who are you then?'

'Emily.' The voice came from behind them both. Carter caught sight of his sleepy daughter standing in the kitchen doorway but before he could order her out she padded further into the room. 'I'm Emily, and you're Dad's boss. We've met before.'

Melanie smiled at Carter over the sheet she was holding. 'You're right, but I'm surprised you remember that.'

Emily thought. 'It wasn't that long ago.'

'You're right, I suppose it wasn't. It's nice to see you again, Emily.'

'And you.' The small child came to a stop in front of Melanie. She threw her father a confident look before extending a hand to the senior officer. A curt laugh erupted from Melanie as she reciprocated the gesture. Meanwhile, Carter was somewhere between proud and deeply embarrassed.

'Melanie's brought you a hot chocolate treat for breakfast,

little bug, but she's told me you can only have it if you're quick getting ready for school.' Carter tried on the lie with a good amount of conviction.

Emily narrowed her eyes and looked from her dad to Melanie before shrugging. 'That seems fair.' Without another word she turned and wandered out of sight.

'It wouldn't have been fair if it was my bloody suggestion,' he said, followed by a chug of coffee. 'Good coffee you've brought here though, boss.'

'Good kid you've got there, Carter,' Melanie said, hopping off the breakfast stool.

He smiled. 'Yeah, she's alright that one, isn't she?'

It was late morning when Melanie pushed her way into the shared office space of her team, clutching a photograph print-out. All of her officers were busy – or at least, they appeared to be. Read was hunched over Morris' desk to scribble something on her notepad – a tech request, Melanie guessed – meanwhile Fairer was in the middle of a phone call, and Carter and Burton looked busy with their own piles of paperwork. But Melanie felt that the card she currently held trumped the lot of them, so she stood in front of their bare evidence board and coughed loudly into the room, catching the attention of Carter and Burton to begin with. Melanie gave Carter the nod to round up the rest of them.

'Oi,' he called.

Read was quick to jump to attention, joining the majority of the team up front. Fairer held up his index finger to beg another moment on his call. 'Thank you, yep, that's great, thanks so much,' he said, putting the phone down as he spoke. 'A friend of Ethan's. Said that Fin bloke had told him what was happening and he wants to come in, see if he can help,' he explained, taking a seat next to Read.

'When's he coming in?' Melanie asked.

'Late afternoon today.'

'Eager?' Carter jumped in.

'Seems to be, but not in a nervous way. I think there's something...' Fairer petered out.

'Be mindful that we won't have Fin in to officially identify Ethan until later today too,' Melanie cautioned, and Fairer nodded his understanding. 'Now we've got that excitement out the way, anyone got anything else they want to share?' Melanie watched her team for reactions; she thought she saw a look between Fairer and Read but neither of them were moved to offer anything so she continued. 'Archer called me into her office to tell me that there's a leak in the team.' She let the statement hang in the air for a second and watched as one by one her colleagues registered the accusation. 'I defended you all, naturally, but Carter went a step further.'

Melanie held the silence for a beat until Carter offered his involvement. 'Boss told me what had happened with an editor of a local paper. He called Archer with information that must have come from someone involved with the case somehow, and he used that not only to convince Archer there was a leak in the department, but that it was a female member of the team who was responsible. We now think it might have been a fishing expedition.'

Melanie carried on. 'Carter went to meet with the editor in the end. He gave Edd a description that doesn't match Morris or Burton, ergo, not a member of our team.'

'So, who was the tosser talking to?' Read asked, grit in his voice.

Melanie turned around to pin her photograph handout to the board behind her. It was a still shot of the woman from the murder tape, standing behind Ethan, the dead man's head resting against the flat of her stomach. There were no distinguishing features in sight.

'It was a woman, northern twang to her accent, five eight, maybe nine,' Melanie said, relaying the description. 'You'll forgive my delay in sharing this with you, folks, but I had to make a pit stop at Waller's office on the way here. I'm not so good with the maths but George knows the size and measurement of Ethan by this point, which gives us a way of working out the size and measurement of the woman standing behind him.'

Carter moved from his standpoint to inspect the picture closer. 'Fuckin' A.'

Burton, as though picking up on her partner's realisation, stared wide-eyed at the image as well. 'The editor met our killer.'

20

Morris tapped her knuckles against the open door of Melanie's office. Melanie's head snapped up, her attention drawn away from Ethan's autopsy report that lay across her desk. She'd already seen Fin Gallagher for a list of additional names and her final few questions, and she'd received the courtesy call from Waller to confirm what they already knew: Yes, it was Ethan Irwill lying on the stretcher.

Fairer had accompanied Gallagher to Waller's office, and on Fairer's return to the station he'd even reported to Melanie how believable Gallagher's reaction had been: 'The bloke looked cut up enough to me,' he said, before pardoning himself for clumsy phrasing.

Melanie had been pawing at the report since, trying to find something more in it that might actually help. She had to hope that Morris might bring with her some workable angles at least. She motioned for her junior to come in, with Read following close behind. Morris clutched a laptop like it was a chest plate of body armour, even as she took a seat opposite her boss. Read didn't have the same nervous disposition as her though; Melanie thought that if anything he seemed excited.

'What's new?' Melanie asked, setting her paperwork to one side.

'We got into Ethan's dark web material,' Morris said, her face finally cracking into a smile. 'Well, Read did.'

'I'm good at guessing passwords.'

'So that's how we got in?' Melanie asked, trying to focus the discussion.

'Through some of the software scrambling I've put together, we were able to see how many characters Ethan's password was.' Morris set the laptop down in the space between her and Melanie to show her superior the password entry field and the series of dots that denoted the password itself. 'There were eleven characters that we needed to guess at.'

'And? Where did you find the password?'

Morris and Read swapped a look of amusement. In the end it was Read who announced: 'Snuffmegood.'

Melanie matched their delight. 'His username?'

'Yep.' Morris hit a key on the laptop and pop-ups packed with conversation scripts unfolded one by one until the screen was overlaid with them. 'We've got everything from their first conversation right through to them swapping emails, phone numbers, and eventually agreeing to take things offline completely.'

'Offline, meaning they started to see each other in person?' Melanie said.

'We haven't had a chance to go through everything yet, but from the conversations we've skimmed it looks as though, yes, they swapped to in-person meet-ups after a while. We've also got phone numbers now so we can match the killer's with Ethan's phone records, to see if we can find out how often they were talking, whether there were texts, codes, anything.'

Melanie nodded along with each point that Morris made. 'Okay, this is – Christ, this is brilliant, you two. I want this work distributed across the team now.' She stood and walked to the doorway. 'Carter, you're up. Wait,' she added, calling to the retreating DCs who turned to face her. 'Morris, what time are you off?'

She looked at her watch. 'Half an hour ago.' She smiled. 'I'll get this stuff finished up and then make a move, I promise.'

Melanie back-stepped into her office, with Carter close behind. 'What have we found?'

'Morris and Read have cracked the dark web software. They've got all of Ethan's conversations with the would-be killer, including details to take things offline. We need mobile numbers to be tracked, conversations to be read through. Get Burton involved?'

Carter nodded. 'Goes without saying. Can you get printouts of the conversations?'

'Nothing leaves this office,' Melanie cautioned. 'Archer is meeting with her editor friend first thing tomorrow morning, allegedly to give him a bollocking but we'll see. Either way, I'm not chancing any accusations getting out. Print it, read it, shred what you don't need. Make sure that Burton and Fairer know that score too.'

'Fairer isn't here, boss, and neither is Burton,' Carter replied. 'They've gone to meet with that chap, the friend of Ethan's who called in. They should be downstairs now.'

'Alright then. Morris will get everything ready for people to start going through before she goes anywhere. For those of us left in the office, this is top priority over anything else now,' Melanie said, filing away the autopsy report. 'I want a pack each for everyone to start on, and we'll see what the other two bring back from the latest buddy when they're done.'

Burton set a small glass of water on the table in front of Scott Kerrick; a well-built man in his early thirties, if Burton had to guess. For someone who had opted to be here, he looked especially nervous, and Burton was suddenly glad of the opportunity to sit in on Fairer's interview with the man. Both detectives had gone through their formal introductions and Burton had complied with the request for something to drink, but she wasn't in the mood for making anyone too comfortable.

'Why is it that you wanted to come in and talk to us, Mr Kerrick?' she asked, taking her seat at the table. 'Did Mr Gallagher mention something in particular to you about the investigation or...' she left the suggestion to hang there while Kerrick chugged down his water.

'Fin told me that it was Ethan, he was sure of it, that Ethan had been murdered and I just – I just thought there must be something I could do.'

'You and Ethan were close?' Fairer asked, his pen hovering over his notebook.

'Closer than he was with the others, I'd like to think at least.'

'You weren't in the list of names that Mr Gallagher originally gave to us,' Burton said, casting an eye over the paper in front of her. 'Why might that be?'

He puckered his lips into something like a smirk. 'Fin and I don't have much good blood between us, but we get on well enough for the good of the group.'

'Anything that might relate to all of this?' Burton asked.

'God no, nothing. There are just some people you don't get along with.'

'And how well did you get along with Ethan?'

'We got on well, always. We never have a bad word between us but Ethan wasn't exactly an open book, not really.'

'What makes you say that?'

'He liked his privacy. We're blokes, you know, it was never a problem.' Kerrick and Fairer shared a knowing look and, in the interest of getting a lead, Burton swallowed down her annoyance and waited for the man to continue. 'But toward the end, over the last few months, Ethan started acting differently. I thought he did, anyway, and one or two of the others.'

'Mr Gallagher didn't mention that,' Burton said.

Kerrick rolled his eyes. 'No, Fin wouldn't. He doesn't tend to notice things unless they're lined up under his nose. But Ethan definitely changed.'

'How so? Are there specific things that you noticed?' Fairer said.

'He'd still come out with us, but he was drinking much less.'

'That's a big change, is it?'

'For Ethan? Definitely. He was on his phone a lot too, taking calls and sending texts. We called him out on it once or twice, but he always said that it was for work.'

'And you don't think it was?' Burton asked.

Kerrick shook his head. 'Look, Ethan didn't tell me a fat lot about it all, so I don't even know how much this will help.'

Burton felt a twist of excitement in the base of her stomach. She shot Fairer a sideward glance to be sure he was ready to note down whatever was coming.

'There was a woman. That's as much as I know, genuinely, but toward the end Ethan told me that there was someone he was involved with – someone he was going out with, that's exactly how he phrased it.'

'He didn't tell you who this woman was?'

'Only that she kept him on a tight leash, but that he liked it.'

'Is that his comment or yours?' Burton clarified.

'His, actually. He said she was a bit out there, like, he could never predict what was coming. I know there were a couple of times when he went home and just found her there.'

'What, waiting for him outside his house?' Fairer pushed.

'No, no, like *in* his house, like she'd gotten in somehow.' Kerrick let out a laugh that was tinged with something like sadness. 'I told him it was weird, but he said he liked it; he liked not knowing what was coming next.'

Fairer picked up with another question but Burton tuned the conversation out. Instead, she pulled out her own notebook and made a comment on the front page, a thought that she hoped forensics would find some use for:

The killer has been inside Ethan's actual house.

If they could match female DNA from the cottage to any female DNA found at Ethan's, they'd be a step closer to pinning something on their suspect – when they found her.

21

It took so long to go through the piles of conversation transcripts and transform them into something meaningful, that Morris had gone and returned with the team hardly noticing. On Monday morning, Melanie was almost surprised when the DC knocked on her open door.

'Did I miss much?'

'We've all been buried under this.' Melanie gestured to the papers in front of her. 'There are some things that Read and Fairer have found along the way, though I think Carter and Burton got quite a mix of good and uninteresting. If there's anything uninteresting about this case.' She almost laughed. 'How about you? Are you a dark web expert?'

Morris hesitated. 'I don't think the tech teams are as far behind on knowledge as the seminar leaders seemed to think they were. The good news is, I get a certificate.' She smiled and Melanie matched the expression.

'We'll get a frame.'

'They're actually emailing them out.'

'Goddamn digital age.' The two shared a quick laugh. 'Go, see how the madding crowd is and what delights they've got for you.' Melanie checked her watch. 'We'll re-group in an hour.'

Domdomdom:
```
How much research have you done?
```
Snuffmegood:
```
Enough to know it's something I want to try
```
Domdomdom:
```
It's not really something you just try, is it?
```
Snuffmegood:
```
I don't know
Isn't it?
```
Domdomdom:
```
There's no coming back from this
You can't decide that you just don't like it
when we've done it
```
Snuffmegood:
```
Well I'll be dead so it won't matter whether I
like it or not
Are you in for this or not?
```
Domdomdom:
```
I don't like that tone
```
Snuffmegood:
```
Yeah well
I don't think I like yours
```

The conversation cut short soon after that, with only a time-stamp showing that both participants had left the private room they'd been talking through. Morris closed the chat window and opened another before turning to address the team. The seats behind her were occupied by Melanie, Carter, Burton and Read;

Fairer was chasing down Ethan's bank details, again, so he'd been excused from the catch-up. Each officer had agreed to compile their findings, to build a bigger picture of their victim and the person they had to assume was their killer. This was the first time everyone was seeing what the others had found

'Credit to Fairer for finding these titbits from really early on in their discussions about all of the snuff business. The tone that's set up here is a good introduction to both of them though, from what Fairer has talked me through.' Melanie noted Morris' willingness to credit her teammate; she wondered whether that was something she'd brought back from the training weekend. 'Their conversation went dead completely for a good three days after this, although we can see from this window that Ethan was still logging into the chat.' Morris turned to move the mouse, hovering the cursor over the parts of the screen that showed four different entries from Ethan, and none from their mystery killer. 'When the other speaker does come back, it's pretty obvious that she expects Ethan to have been waiting for her.'

Domdomdom:
Had time to tweak that attitude yet?
Snuffmegood:
I think we got off on the wrong terms
Domdomdom:
That's one way of putting it

'It's idle flirtation for the next few hours, to be honest with you,' Morris said, again turning back to the crowd.

Melanie could feel the beginnings of some confidence in her team; this new information was good stuff. And then there was Scott Kerrick's reveal of a new girlfriend. This was another line to follow, given that the girlfriend and the killer might have been one and the same.

Melanie had ordered a second forensics sweep of Ethan's house over the weekend, focusing on drains, washing – clean and dirty – and bed linens, looking for any nook or cranny where female DNA might be hiding.

Meanwhile, while Read and Fairer had read through their share of conversations. The pair had also spent a handful of hours apiece re-reading Ethan's bank statements for anything they'd missed the first time around – anything that might show them where Ethan's killer-cum-girlfriend liked to shop, eat, or buy her murder materials from.

'Carter, you're up,' Morris said, clicking to the next conversation and sidestepping out of the way. As Morris took her seat, Carter came to the front of the room.

'I got some really fun stuff,' he said, with raised eyebrows. Carter scrolled low enough for a conversation clip to hang on the screen behind him, but he gave the team the edited version of the full script. 'They start talking about sex pretty soon after they make up from that minor spat.'

'So, I miss all the good stuff,' Morris said with a smirk.

'They don't talk sexually with each other, as such, but there's a lot of talk about what they enjoy, what they've done, what they'd still like to do.'

'Is there anything incriminating in among it all?' Melanie asked.

'Funny you should ask.' Carter turned the mouse wheel to bring up a later stretch of dialogue which he'd highlighted for ease of access.

Domdomdom:
```
You're cocky now but you won't be when the
time comes
They're always scared at the end
```

'Ethan isn't her first.'

'It doesn't sound like it from this part of their talk, no,' Carter said, leaning against the desk behind him. 'After this there's a fair amount of talk about preferences, but rather than sexual there's a lot of violence. At one point she asks whether Ethan has ever imagined how he'd like it to happen.'

'And?'

Snuffmegood:
```
I don't know
Strangled, poisoned, something that I can't
see coming, you know
But really, I feel like that would be your
choice not mine
```

Burton rubbed a hand from her forehead down over her face. 'Is anyone else having their bloody minds blown by this entire thing? Like, this is next level stuff, is it not?'

'Easy there, Burton,' Carter said, his tone more playful than that of his partner.

'She's not wrong, Edd,' Read joined. 'It's pretty fucking extra.'

'Before we all lose our heads, can we deal with the rest of these conversations?' Melanie said, trying to encourage focus in the team. But she could see from their expressions that their grasp on the case was slipping, and she couldn't exactly blame them. 'Why don't we take ten minutes? Grab coffee, shout at each other in the corridor, do what you need to do. I'll check in with Fairer.' As Melanie finished speaking the door cracked open and in walked the man himself. 'Perfect timing.'

As Burton stood from the seating area, she gave her superior a nod and a thin smile, to express gratitude Melanie assumed, although the break was as much for her as it was for the team.

'Any news, Fairer?'

He came and stood alongside his boss. 'I didn't find anything relating to the girlfriend, as such, but I did find this.' He lifted a bank statement to show Melanie a highlighted entry dating back three and a half months. 'We didn't know what we were looking for the first time around so it was easy to miss I guess, but MacArthur and Russel are a solicitor's firm based in the centre of town.'

Melanie followed the name of the payee along to the amount paid. 'I see. So, what was our Ethan paying them the sum of £350 for?'

22

Melanie tapped her pen against the notepad in front of her and checked her watch again. She'd arrived at the forensics offices without warning, admittedly, but it felt like another bad sign that she'd been kept waiting so long. It had been nearly fifteen minutes since she'd been shown to Graham's office, and the forensics expert still hadn't shown his face.

Melanie took her phone from her pocket to check for messages from the team, but the digital clock was the only thing there to greet her. She'd hoped there would be something back at base at least; a solicitor's number, if not a meeting scheduled. She thought again of what a man like Ethan might be paying a solicitor for, for such an amount as well. There weren't any charges against him, ongoing or prior, and they hadn't found paperwork relating to a mortgage, or anything else he owed or owned. Melanie opened a fresh web browser on her phone to test out one last idea just as the door swung open and in stepped Graham, a pale blue evidence folder pressed to his chest with less filling than Melanie had hoped for.

She stood to greet him. 'Graham.'

'DI Watton, always a pleasure, never a chore,' he smiled, taking a seat at his desk.

Melanie held back a wince. 'That can't be a good sign.'

'What can't?'

'Opening with a compliment. Does that mean you don't have anything for me, or do I really look as tired as I feel and you're being kind?'

Graham narrowed his eyes. 'There's no right answer to that question, I'm sure of it.' When Melanie didn't offer any guidance on how to respond, Graham turned his attention to the folder he'd brought in with him. He opened it and let sheets of paper fall loose onto his desk before he started skimming through them. 'Do you want the good news or the bad first?'

'Any news, I'll take what I can get.'

'Okay, we've got a DNA match from the crime scene with the house. We took your advice, although I like to think we would have got there anyway.' He paused here to glance up at Melanie with a quick smirk. 'When we pulled samples from the drains around the place, we found some long brown hair which obviously didn't belong to the victim. We matched it with the samples we'd pulled from around the crime scene house, so we can definitively say that the same woman was at both locations.'

'Okay, that's a start. What's the bad news?'

'Maybe bad news, I should have softened it a little. We found a third sample in the crime scene house and when we ran it through our system it came back as an unknown female.' He handed Melanie the results for her to scan through. 'The most likely possibility is that it was left over from a previous visitor, and the cleaning company didn't do a good enough job of getting rid of things. We haven't found traces of this unknown female anywhere in the victim's actual house, so our leading theory is that she's a no one, but it wouldn't be right if I didn't mention it.' He took the sheet back from Melanie and set it to one side.

'I appreciate that.'

'The hair is the only trace of our mystery murderer woman in the victim's actual home though. If she was there, she did a mighty fine job of getting rid of herself.'

'No prints?'

'No anything. We have a patchwork of prints from the crime scene house; it looks as though some of them she wiped clean, some she didn't. Either way, the prints we found there we can't match to a single thing at the victim's actual home, and we combed the place.'

'I don't understand.' Melanie leaned back in her seat and ran a hand through her hair. 'Why would she get rid of herself at the home, but not at the murder scene?'

Graham shrugged. 'You have her on camera at the scene, near as damn it at least, which makes it impossible to dispute that she was there. Maybe she wants to be able to say she was never at the house?'

'But why? It doesn't make any sense.'

'I'm afraid that's not my area, DI Watton, it's yours.' He smiled. 'Whatever her reason for doing it, it's moot. We can put her in both houses at one time or another, which is a positive, surely. There were one or two other things that we pulled from the scene, medications that were left in the kitchen, one of which was a sedative; Waller has already told us his suspicions insofar as the victim being drugged so that tallies up.'

'Was there a name on the prescription?'

'Your victim's.'

Melanie sighed. 'Of course.'

'I'm guessing you're hitting a lot of dead ends?'

'Like you wouldn't believe.' She flashed her colleague an

apologetic glance. 'I'm sorry, this isn't your area, I know. Is there anything else from the crime scene?'

'I wish there was something more but there wasn't anything that we didn't expect. We can place her there, if only we knew who she was. But we're ready as soon as you've got a comparative sample for us.'

'If you were to find anything else from woman number two...' Melanie petered out.

'I'd call personally.'

'Thanks, Graham.'

'Any time.' He stood as Melanie did and walked to the door in time to open it for her. 'Don't kill yourself over this, okay? You'll get there.'

So everyone seems to believe, Melanie thought, before she thanked her colleague again and stepped out into the hallway.

By the time Melanie had reached the car park she felt deflated – by the case, by the lack of leads, by not knowing who to even turn to. Graham was right, she knew that much; something would turn up eventually, but the waiting period was a killer itself. She pushed her key fob into the opening for it, pressed down on the clutch and started her engine, just as her mobile phone hummed in her pocket. Melanie left the handbrake on as she pulled the handset out and check the message preview:

Chris Burton: Got through to the solicitor. Appointment with him at 9am tomorrow.

Melanie dropped her forehead against the steering wheel. 'Thank Christ for that.'

The following morning, Carter rushed from his front door, his hands fumbling with his tie as he walked. He climbed into the passenger seat of Burton's car and felt the tug of the vehicle when he'd barely closed the door behind him.

'Is there a rush on that I don't know about?' he asked.

Burton kept her eyes on the road. 'I just want to get there in good time.'

'We've got thirty minutes and it's a ten-minute drive, Chris.'

'We might not be able to park.'

Carter opened his mouth to counter-argue but from the look of his partner's blank profile, he thought better of it. 'So, is there a pool going on what the solicitor will be for?'

'Mel wondered whether there might be property we haven't found yet.'

Carter frowned. 'Doesn't seem likely though, does it?'

'She's reaching, isn't she, like the rest of us.' Burton took a corner too fast and both of them veered to the left before righting themselves. 'Sorry, Edd. I think her other theory is that the bloke might be holding documents for Ethan, if there was something he didn't want left in the house for any reason.'

'Okay, sure, I'd buy that.'

There was a comfortable silence then until Burton rounded the corner into the street where the offices were based. She slowly crawled along until she spotted the right number and then parallel parked immediately outside of the building. It was too early for the street to be busy in this part of the city centre. Burton killed the engine and glanced at the clock on the dashboard.

'Good job we gave ourselves plenty of time, eh?' Carter said.

Burton threw him a look and spotted his smile. 'Alright, Sarcasmo, I'm eager, so sue me.'

'We're in the right place for it.'

Both officers agreed they'd push their luck and try for an

early start. They climbed out of the vehicle and walked to the office together, but found the door locked.

'Come on, it's eight forty-five, you're telling me no one's here,' Carter said.

Burton nodded behind him. 'Someone is.'

'I'm afraid we don't open for another fifteen minutes, sir.' The woman at the door was receptionist material. She had an air of importance that she didn't necessarily deserve. Her hair was pulled tight back away from her face, and her heels were of a height that meant she couldn't possibly do much walking. Carter recognised a gatekeeper when he saw one. He pulled out his warrant card and pressed it against the glass.

'We're here to see Mr Yarbury, we've got an appointment.'

The woman fell over herself to assist the pair of them then. Doors were held open, drinks were offered, and in the end Carter had to insist they were taken to Mr Yarbury's office. 'Of course, of course,' the woman replied, but it was still another three minutes before they were walking through the man's door.

'Mr Yarbury, I'm DS Carter and this is my colleague DC Burton, I believe you spoke on the phone together yesterday.' Formal handshakes were exchanged between the three of them before Carter and Burton took seats opposite the solicitor.

'You're here about Ethan Irwill, correct?'

Carter found the man's formality a little disarming. 'Correct.' But he tried to match his tone. 'We've been going through his bank records and there was a recent payment made out to this firm. The woman that my colleague initially spoke to, I assume the lady out front?' Yarbury confirmed this. 'She informed DC Burton that you were the solicitor dealing with Ethan.'

'She informed you correctly.' The man flashed a tight smile before shifting around folders that were in front of him. 'After we spoke yesterday, DC Burton, I went to the trouble of searching out Ethan's folder, on the assumption that you'd like it as part of your investigation.' Burton reached out to take the documents the man was now holding but he pulled them closer to his chest, in what looked to Carter to be a defensive gesture. 'Mr Irwill has passed away, is that correct?'

'That's correct,' Burton said. 'This will contribute toward his murder investigation.'

'Nasty business.'

'Quite nasty, yes,' Carter said, throwing Burton a quick glance. 'You'll understand that we're eager to get everything we can that might help with our investigation.'

'Of course, of course. Unfortunately, officer, I'll need permission from Mr Irwill's family before I'm able to copy any of this information for you.'

'Ah, there's the problem. You'll know from those documents, I assume, that Ethan had no family to speak of. Surely that negates the need for you to request permission from them?' Carter asked, his tone a little lighter in the hope that it might soften the man, but he didn't take the bait.

Yarbury parted the folder, peered inside, then closed it. 'We at least need to make an attempt to contact the executor before we allow you to take copies, DS Carter, I'm afraid. It's company protocol and in Mr Irwill's memory it seems only fair.'

Carter caught Burton's eye again and gave her a narrowed look. 'I'm sorry,' he said, turning back to face Yarbury. 'We're yet to confirm what Ethan Irwill was seeing you for, but an executor sounds like…' he trailed off as Yarbury held up a palm.

'My apologies, I'm getting in front of myself. Of course, I can't give you the contents of Mr Irwill's documents until I have permission from the individual named within them. You understand?' Yarbury waited for agreement from each officer, as though he were talking to very young children. 'I can confirm what Mr Irwill was under my consultation for though, yes. Some months back, Mr Irwill came to see me regarding his will.'

'An existing will that he wanted updated?' Carted asked.

'No, no. He didn't yet have one, but he told me that he needed one.'

'Needed one?' Burton said, latching onto the phrasing. 'That's how he put it?'

'Yes, he needed one, he told me, as a matter of urgency...'

23

Domdomdom:
You think you're ready to meet
Snuffmegood:
Well, we'll have to eventually, right
Domdomdom:
It seems a little soon
Snuffmegood:
Nervous?
Because I think it's sweet if you are
Domdomdom:
I'm not. Like I said, it seems a little soon.
Why don't we email for a while first, and see
how things go?
Snuffmegood:
How will that be any different to talking
here?
Domdomdom:
It gives us time to get to know each
other more
Plus, it gives you time to change your mind

Snuffmegood:

Which I won't

Domdomdom:

I think it's sweet that you think you won't

Snuffmegood:

Do you want to meet me or not

Domdomdom:

There's a place that I like to go to in town.
A little coffee shop.

Morris burst into her superior's office without knocking, copies of the conversation transcripts clutched in one hand. Melanie wore a look of surprise and slight irritation – 'Edd, gimme five minutes and I'll call you back.' – as she ended her phone call and gestured to the seat opposite her own. 'Come on then, Morris, what's so urgent?' Melanie said, her tone lightening.

'They met before, earlier than we thought they did.'

'What do you know?'

Morris leaned forward in her seat to spread the sheets out in front of her boss, and Melanie matched the gesture.

'I've been reading through more of their conversations, and this one took place a week and a half before we saw them swap emails. Ethan starts talking about meeting in person and she, they, whoever.' Morris' voice was hurried with excitement. 'She tries to delay it, I don't fully know why, she seems to think he'll change his mind – I don't know. Anyway, there's a place mentioned.' She pointed to a highlighted strip of conversation on the third page.

Domdomdom:

Do you know Benny's, in town?

'She says it's somewhere she likes to go, boss. You know what that means?'

'It means she might be a regular.' Melanie stood as she spoke and popped her head out of the open doorway. 'Read, Fairer, a minute.' By the time Melanie was back at her desk both officers had stepped into the room. 'Morris here has got us a lead. Do either of you know Benny's in town?'

'Best kept secret,' Read said with a smile. 'They do crackin' toasties there.'

'They might also be harbouring our missing murderer.' Melanie lifted the offending sheet of paper and stretched it toward Fairer, who took it from her. 'It sounds as though our woman might have been something of a regular, and she definitely arranged to meet Ethan there at least once from the looks of this. Can you head over there as soon as you've finished whatever you're working on?'

Fairer nodded. 'One or two final forms for interviews with Ethan's friends.'

'It won't take longer than thirty minutes, then we'll head out.'

'Take a few pictures of Ethan,' Melanie said. 'Anything to jog their memories.'

Read and Fairer pushed through into the bustling café. Both of them had expected to miss the lunchtime rush but it looked as though they were in the thick of it. Every table in the place was occupied and there was still a queue snaking round the room, trailing back toward the entryway. Fairer nudged his partner.

'How good must these bloody toasties be?'

Read gave a curt laugh. 'Not good enough to stop us from finding a manager.' He started to ease his way through the crowd with a series of, 'Excuse me,' and, 'Don't mind me,' and Fairer dutifully followed, but after two minutes of pushing and shoving Read's patience finally ran short. 'Police,' he announced to the room. 'Police, trying to get through here.'

Fairer's face flushed and he raised a hand to partially cover his shamed expression, but he followed his partner all the same until the pair of them reached the counter. A young woman, who had been serving hungry office-workers until a few seconds ago, threw the detectives a startled expression as they reached her.

'Is the manager about?' Read said.

'Right here,' came a voice from behind them.

Read and Fairer turned around to the sight of a middle-aged man with a friendly expression and open arms, as though he were displaying himself. The welcoming gesture gave a clear view of his rotund stomach, covered by a shirt that looked fit to burst. He closed the small gap between himself and the officers before talking, and this time held out a hand as he spoke.

'I'm Albert, Alby to friends.' He shook hands with each officer in turn. 'How can I help the fine boys in blue this afternoon?'

'We're actually looking to track down someone who we think might be a regular customer here,' Fairer explained, pulling the picture of Ethan from his inside pocket. 'We don't have a picture of the woman herself.'

'But we have reason to believe that she brought this man here,' Read explained as Fairer handed over the picture.

The image was entirely different to the one that had been circulated on the news. The press image had shown a drugged and distressed Ethan, likely recognisable only to those closest to him. Meanwhile the picture they had now – lifted from Ethan's own home – showed a young and fresh-faced man on a night out with friends. Ethan wore a clean white shirt and a smile that matched it, and Alby took his time looking over the image.

'Sure, I know this guy. Something with an E, right? He came in with a lady a few times. I don't know that I'd call her a regular, that said, but sure–'

'How often did you see them together?' Read said, cutting off the ramble before it could gain traction.

'Probably a handful of times? I remember seeing her on her own once or twice too.'

'In the last week or so, would you say?' Fairer pushed.

'No, no, not that recently. It's been a good couple of weeks since I remember seeing either of them. But, you know, I don't live in the shop, so you're welcome to ask the staff who are in today whether they recognise the guy from recently.'

'Thanks, Alby, we'll get right on that.' Fairer tucked the image away for safekeeping. 'You'd know the woman if you saw her again, do you think?'

'Sure. If I had the time I'd try to find her on security.'

Read and Fairer swapped a glance before Read asked, 'You have footage of her?'

Alby gestured to one corner and then another. The officers followed the manager's sightline and spotted two cameras tucked away in opposing ends of the room.

'We don't wipe tapes anymore. Everything is saved digitally.' He chuckled. 'You'd think the police would know that.'

Fairer tried to match the manager's light-heartedness. 'We're a little slow on the uptake. Do you think we could get a copy of those recordings, Alby? Would there be any problem with handing those over?'

'For the police? No problem at all. It'll take a little while though. Like I said, boys, it's been at least two or three weeks since I saw the woman and we get a good amount of foot traffic even on our slow days.'

'We can wait while you pull footage for the last month or so,' Fairer said, his tone tight.

'Well alright then, you give me ten minutes or so and I'll see what I can do. Meantime, show my Maria that picture of yours, would you? Tell her to fix you a couple of lunchtime special toasties while you're at it. We offer a good discount for you folks who are keeping the city safe.'

Read gave the manager a wide grin. 'Don't mind if we do.'

24

Carter was the last into the briefing room that morning. He brought with him a bag bursting full of breakfast sandwiches, which softened the blow of his late arrival. He threw bacon and egg combinations in the direction of Read and Fairer before chucking Burton a double egg and, dropping to one knee in a theatrical fashion, he held up the final sandwich to Melanie.

'Good leader, I beg your forgiveness,' he said, his tone jovial. 'I come bringing offerings of runny egg on rye.'

Melanie took the sandwich. 'I'll eat the sandwich, Carter, but you don't have to be so bloody chirpy about it.' Despite her tone, she smiled as she took the offering and set it on the empty desk next to her. 'Custody weekend?' she said quietly as Carter stood. He nodded with some enthusiasm. 'Well, that explains everything then. Pull up a pew; chew quietly.'

Carter took his seat, his own sandwich in tow, and tucked into his breakfast along with the rest of the team. Meanwhile, Melanie turned to write on the board behind her. In the centre of the disconcertingly empty space she wrote: *woman?* She drew rigid lines branching off from this middle point, and at the end of each she wrote all they knew: *dark web, local, coffee shop, not her first time doing this.* Melanie capped the pen and turned back to her team.

'I want this board full. What do we know?'

'The coffee shop owner understands he's to call us when and if this woman shows up again.' Read spoke through a mouthful of crust. 'He said it's been a while since he saw her, longer than she's gone before. But there must be something significant about that place for her to have taken Ethan there in the first place, right?'

'She must at least feel comfortable there. Maybe she trusts the staff?' Burton said.

'Or maybe she thought the staff wouldn't notice her,' Melanie added. 'Can this owner give us a better description than the one he gave at the first meeting?'

Fairer shook his head. 'He reckons there's nothing unusual about her. Average height, dark hair, pretty enough.'

'That's the beauty of her though I suppose, isn't it?' Fairer met Burton's question with a frown so she explained, 'Who's going to notice her? If that's how people are describing her, then who is going to see her against any other average height, dark haired woman? Christ, boss, he could be describing either of us with something that vague.'

Melanie frowned. 'You'd describe me as "pretty enough"?' Burton opened her mouth to defend herself but Melanie held up a palm. 'I take your point. There's nothing to help her stand out from the crowd. We have the security footage to go through?' she directed the question to Read and Fairer, the latter of whom leapt to answer.

'We're going through them file by file for some old-fashioned detective work, but we sent them over to Morris–'

'Where is Morris?' Melanie scanned the room.

'She's working with the tech team today to try to crack a hidden lead on Ethan's laptop, but they're also going to try a trick or two with the footage to see if they can get any results faster than we can.'

'Which seems likely given how much footage there is,' Read added.

'Why are we assuming she's local?' Carter asked, nodding towards the board.

'How many of you knew about Benny's before three days ago?' Melanie replied. Read raised his hand but no one else responded. 'If she isn't local, then she at least knows the city well enough to know some of its best haunts.'

'Or some of the least known ones,' Carter said between mouthfuls. 'If we're assuming she uses locations where she thinks she won't be noticed or remembered.'

Melanie ran a hand through her hair and turned back to the board. 'The fact of the matter is that we're this far in and we know fuck all about this woman, do we?'

'That's not entirely true.' Archer's voice rang out from the back of the room, catching the entire team off guard. Melanie turned at once to greet her. 'Ian Tatham, my editor friend, and I have had a good old chat, on account of him trying to scam us – me.' She crossed the room and gestured for the board marker Melanie was holding. 'May I?'

'Please.' She handed over the pen and took a seat with her colleagues.

'Firstly, the woman changes her accent.' *Northern but hint of west midlands on certain words.* Archer added information to the board as she spoke, piece by piece. 'Ian said that over the course of their conversation there were vowel slips and unique sounds coming out left, right and centre, which doesn't help us to narrow down our search as such, but at least we know some ticks to look out for. He said she seems confident when she enters a room.' *Carries herself well. Maintains eye contact.* 'But that there were times when he questioned her information and she was visibly perturbed by his interruptions.' *Non-confrontational?*

'How so? Did he say what she actually did?' Melanie asked.

'He said she stuttered.' *Stammer when nervous?* 'He also said she claimed to be a uniformed officer who wasn't involved in the investigation but had heard someone in this room discussing it publicly, and that's where her information came from.'

'Which is total bollo–'

'Yes, we're quite aware of what it is, DS Carter.'

'And she didn't show him any ID, that much we know already,' Melanie added. 'I assume he confirmed that with you?'

Archer nodded. 'He said he suspected she wasn't actually an officer but, in his own words, he thought he'd try his luck to be sure.' She spoke through nearly gritted teeth; her frustration at the situation made her words taut. 'I appreciate it's not a huge amount of information, but they're specific details you won't gather up from security footage and snuff films, so at least they're more particular than what you've got already.'

'No, ma'am, this is useful information to have. These are things we can look out for.' Melanie closed the gap between herself and her superior. 'Is that everything you could squeeze out of him?'

Archer smiled. 'Near as damn it, but he's downstairs with a sketch artist as we speak so there's hope for the weasel yet.'

'She didn't have a fringe as such, it was more like there'd been a fringe there some months back and she was growing it out. Do you see what I mean?'

The sketch artist nodded along with Tatham's description and added in a small wisp of hair either side of the woman's centre parting. Each piece of hair became fashioned into a small wave as Tatham described the growth in more detail and the artist, with a sigh and another amendment, added further niceties to the image he was compiling. Alongside the traditional sketch artist there sat a digital artist, building a matching structure on a computer screen. Tatham looked back and forth between the images before providing the next snippet.

'I'm actually not sure what colour her eyes were. It's hard to recall now, although they were certainly dark. Brown at a guess, although it's hard to be...' he trailed off as he eyed the images in front of him. 'It would make sense for them to be brown, I suppose, given the darkness of her hair. Why don't we try brown?'

The artist darkened the eyes of the compilation image and the digital worker matched the change. The computer screen showed a clearer image though, the digital interpretation showing the fine details of hazel, darker hazel.

'Maybe black, even?' Tatham pushed.

The digital artist let out a huff of air. 'Only if she was wearing contacts.'

'Well, maybe she was.'

Archer pushed the door open with a force. After three minutes of observing from the other side of the office window, she'd seen enough to know that Tatham had given them as much as he was likely to.

'It looks to me like you've given us a fair description of the woman who approached you, Ian, so why don't we call it a day there?' Despite posing it as a question, Archer's tone revealed it to be more of a statement.

Tatham stood and assessed the results from a different angle. 'So that's your killer?'

'No, that's the woman who's passing herself off as a police officer. They're two very different things.' Archer closed the gap between herself and the editor. She squeezed his elbow joint gently to catch his attention and when he turned to face her, she continued, 'Incidentally, if that accusation makes it into print, we'll be coming after you for libel – as well as obstruction. Are we on the same page there?'

Tatham forced out a huff of air that could have been a laugh. 'Beverley, please. You're really coming after me for a little fun like this? You wouldn't get a thing to stick.'

Archer matched her adversary's smugness. 'No? Okay, Ian, try me.'

25

Carter slumped down on the sofa. He used his fingertip to mop up the spilled cola that was running down the side of his glass, drawing a line in the condensation as it went. He chugged a greedy amount before setting it down on the table in front of him. When he'd got home from work, he'd seen a missed call from Trish with no voicemail left behind. It couldn't have been important, otherwise there would have been something else – a second call, a text, a child on his doorstep. But it crossed his mind collecting Emily from school tomorrow might not be as easy as he'd hoped.

Melanie had given them all strict instructions to be in at the crack of dawn the following day. She'd asked Carter to use his new-found connections in missing persons to run the sketch print of their maybe-killer through the system. 'We've got no reason to think she's missing, I know, but something might stick,' Melanie said, and Carter agreed. Their next step was to officially distribute the sketch of the woman to the public, which meant that, despite Carter's plans to leave early in the afternoon to collect Emily, he would have an uncomfortably long day ahead of him made

138

up of press releases, phone calls, and unpleasant journalists.

'Christ sake,' he said, leaning forward to grab at his drink. He wished it was something stronger, but since he started living alone he'd operated on a strict no-booze policy in the house – for his own good, as well as in case of emergencies.

Carter took another chug of his drink before setting it down and picking up the television remote. He flicked through soap operas, late night shopping shows and settled eventually on the news. He sighed, knowing soon enough his own face would be back in front of blinking bulbs while journalists interrogated Melanie on the release of the new image – but he knew he'd be there to support her, no matter the late-night news re-runs his face would end up on. Suddenly the second murder investigation in an eighteen-month period didn't seem as exciting as it had to begin with. His finger was poised to change the channel again until one announcement was overlaid with another…

'…we've been alerted to an ongoing investigation that is supposedly being hushed up by our very own police force. Viewers, we've been advised to caution you. The next ten minutes of the show may be especially troubling, and not suitable for viewers below the age of 18.'

'Shit.'

Melanie stared from one end of her dining table to the other. On the right-hand side were re-prints of the photographs they had of Ethan; they showed him at slightly different ages now and, as she scanned ahead to the final image, in slightly different states of living. It was hard to believe the man pictured lying on the slab was the same man she could see, two images away, draped around the shoulders of a friend, their faces flushed with alcohol. If she looked especially hard from one version to the another, she could see the slightest of similarities. But it was clear that a lot had happened from one image to the next, and Melanie was growing impatient with not being able to work out exactly what it was. She pinched at the bridge of her nose with her thumb and forefinger, before she shifted her stare to the opposite end of the space, where the sketched and digitised versions of their maybe-murderer were lying next to each other.

'There needs to be more on your end of the table,' she spoke to the image.

After another ten minutes she admitted defeat for the evening. Melanie trod from her dining room to her kitchen, where she pulled cold pasta from the fridge. The large container held enough for the week; or, at least, it had when she'd filled it three days ago. If the copycat case had taught Melanie anything it was to be efficient with time management, and making dinner every evening hardly seemed important when there was a killer on the loose.

Melanie shovelled a generous forkful of food into her mouth and managed one chew before her mobile started to hum from her jeans pocket.

'What?' she said, her curtness muffled by the soft pasta.

'You need to turn on Channel Four.'

Melanie swallowed. 'Why, what's on?'

'Boss, please, just go and turn on your television,' Carter said, his tone pulling tight over the words. 'You need to see what's happening.'

Melanie rushed from the kitchen and into the living room and picked up the remote control. The television took longer than it should have done to turn on, as though weeks of underuse had slowed the machine down. But when the black screen gave way to the first colour images Melanie clicked three times in rapid succession to arrive at the right channel, and there it was, nearing its end now – the footage of Ethan Irwill being murdered.

'Mel, are you there? Did you see it?'

Melanie watched as the video faded to black and was replaced with the image of a news anchor sitting inside the safety of a studio. 'Again, we apologise for anyone who may have been affected by this footage. The video was sent to us this afternoon, as well as to several other news outlets, we've since discovered–'

'Fucking brilliant,' Melanie said, cutting the television's power.

'Do we have a plan for this?'

Melanie dropped onto the sofa behind her and rested her forehead against the palm of her hand. She needed to think. 'Give me a second, Edd.' *There was always a chance of this happening*, she reminded herself. 'It could be anyone that's leaked this, anyone who had a copy of it, and we never knew for certain how widespread the footage was.'

'I hear that, Mel, but that's not what the guy said.'

'What do you mean?'

'He said it was sent to them, and several others. That doesn't sound like someone doing it for money, or someone who's been paid off.'

Melanie considered Carter's line of thought. 'You're guessing it's the woman again?'

'We can't rule it out, I don't think.'

'Archer is going to want a press conference on this as soon as possible,' Melanie said, her tone falling back toward something more professional. 'Can you be good to go on that first thing in the morning? We'll try to get it arranged for just after lunch.'

Carter hesitated. 'Sure, sure I can be ready, whenever.'

And Melanie heard it. 'I'll get you out of the office on time, Carter, don't worry.'

'I'm sorry, boss, obviously I'm there for whatever you need–'

'Don't say sorry for caring about things outside of work,' Melanie said, her eyes flicking toward her dining room. She thought of the images laid out and even now she wondered what she'd be adding there the following day. 'We'll approach different news channels from tomorrow onward, each pair can get in touch with a station. Burton can start with this lot, Channel Four local; she can handle them on her own while we're getting ready for the shitstorm.'

'Okay, Burton will be fine with that.'

'First thing, get Morris to put together copies of the digital and sketch woman that we've got from today, would you? Make sure everyone has one for when they visit the news stations, but tell them all to be mindful of how much information they're giving away, would you?'

'Right, and where are you going to be?'

Melanie rubbed a hand over her face. 'Whether I like it or not, I suspect I'll be in Archer's office. Unless some kind soul fancies swapping places with me.'

Carter dropped a curt laugh down the line that was greeted with silence from his superior. 'Arses, I'm sorry. Were you being serious?'

'Only if you're going to say yes.'

26

Archer chugged her coffee like a thirsty teenager would a pint of lager. She placed the cup down with a gentle thud and wiped at the corners of her mouth. Placing her hands flat on her desk, she pushed herself into a standing position, in synchronicity with her phone starting to ring. She leaned forward to look at the caller display.

'We've got time for you to take that, if you need to,' Melanie said.

Archer pressed a button and silenced the phone. 'One fire at a time.'

The two women stepped out of the office to find Carter waiting outside for them.

'Got your gloves on?' he said, mimicking a one-two punch.

Melanie turned to their superior. 'Forgive him, ma'am, he's always like this on a Friday.'

Archer cracked a tight smile. 'At least one of us is going in ready for a fight.'

The three officers walked the corridors in silence until they arrived outside the room designated for the afternoon's press conference. After the reveal of the video footage on every local television station – and some global ones, Melanie had heard from Read – it hadn't taken much convincing to get the press representatives from newspapers, magazines and God only knew where else to come into the station at short notice. Archer and Melanie had spent most of the morning discussing tactics and they'd agreed that defending their earlier decisions – hiding the tape, shielding Ethan's identity – were their biggest weak spots for this first round of questioning. They had batted potential queries back and forth to each other until their explanations had run dry and they felt ready for that avenue of interrogation at least. But it was the other questions the press might poke with that Melanie found worrying.

'Are we ready?' Archer said, her hand flat against the door, braced to push.

Melanie and Carter nodded and followed Archer into the room. Before the three had even arrived at their positions along the table there were bulbs snapping. Once seated, Melanie could see the usual suspects – including Heather Shawly who, rather than standing tall at the back of the room, was on the front row. For the sake of formality, the officers took their turns introducing themselves before the conference officially started, with Archer launching into a summary of their investigations so far.

'So, you've known from the beginning you were dealing with authentic footage of an actual murder taking place?' a young reporter said from somewhere in the middle of the room.

'It became clear to us early in the investigation that the footage was real, yes,' Melanie said, her tone flat, calm, controlled.

'But you decided to lie about the victim's actual role, in an investigation that you made up entirely to–' Heather Shawly started, but Melanie cut across her.

'We launched a fishing expedition into Ethan Irwill's identity, yes. We didn't want to cause public concern over an investigation that was very much in its infancy when we hadn't been able to determine Mr Irwill's identity in full nor his full involvement in the case.'

'His involvement seems quite clear from the tape,' Heather replied.

Melanie bit back on the comment she desperately wanted to say and opted for something more appropriate. 'Mr Irwill could have been complicit in a fake video for all we knew initially, which is why we sought out his identity in a way that seemed appropriate and safe for public concern at the time.'

'At the time?' Another familiar face latched onto Melanie's phrasing. 'Can we infer from that that you'd behave differently if you were to repeat the early stages of the case?'

Melanie and Archer swapped a side glance; this was something they were ready for.

'Hindsight is a wonderful thing, Mr Kaplan. With hindsight, we would of course act in a different way, knowing what we know now. I don't think being human can be held against us though,' Archer said, her tone surprisingly playful. There was a movement of stifled amusement around the room which she continued to talk across. 'When it comes to making difficult decisions, there are a lot of people who would change them after the fact. That said, given that DI Watton and her team acted in the most appropriate way at the time, with the information they had, it seems redundant now to question her motives, no?' She spoke directly to the journalist in question, who thinned his lips and raised an eyebrow by way of a response.

'Who's the woman then? We know about Irwill, who's the girl with him?' The question rose from the back of the room and Melanie didn't wait to identify the speaker before answering.

'Well, that's what we'd like to know. We're distributing her image across newspapers, local and national, and we're showing the same image to the owners of what we believe to be some of her regular haunts around the city. The photograph is going everywhere it possibly can and we have operatives ready and willing to take calls from the public–'

'So, you're turning to the public again?' Heather cut in.

Melanie opened her mouth to respond but Archer held up a hand to stop her. Archer covered the microphone positioned in front of her and leaned a little further across the table that separated her from the front row of seats.

'I've had you thrown out of a press conference before, Heather. It's going to get embarrassing if you make a habit of this.' Archer uncovered the microphone and leaned back in her seat. 'Are there any other questions from the room?'

'That wasn't the shitstorm that it could have been,' Carter said, holding the door open for Melanie to step back into their office space. 'Archer seemed confident enough with it all.'

'When doesn't that woman seem confident?' Melanie said, turning. 'I can't face the Post-it notes from nutters who think that woman is someone who cut them up on a shopping aisle earlier. Do you want to go and grab a coffee?'

'Can coffee wait? We've got something here,' Read shouted from his desk to the doorway. His hand was clasped over the speaker of his phone, but he quickly returned to the conversation. 'No, no, Mr Yarbury, we fully appreciate that you aren't obliged to divulge these details. ... Yes, yes the video does change matters. I imagine my colleagues didn't feel that they could reveal such sensitive information when they met with you. ... No, of course.'

Melanie and Carter crossed the room to Fairer who was hovering behind his partner.

'The solicitor called?' Carter asked.

'They've been on the phone for ages.' Fairer fidgeted with the collar of his shirt, loosening it with two fingers as though he might be sweating. 'From what I can gather, the bloke has opened the will to try to find information about Irwill's family and anyone named, because he can't track down whoever the executor actually is.'

'And he called us because of that?' Melanie said.

'No, he called us because he wants us to have the will.'

'We understand that you're providing us with these details as a courtesy, yes.' Read held his phone to one ear and cupped his hand around the other, as though physically shutting out the conversation happening around him.

'Tosser,' Carter said, grabbing a chair to sit alongside Read.

'We can actually send a courier over this afternoon if that suits you? We'd like to keep this information as confidential and as secure as possible, you understand, I'm sure. ... Yes, absolutely.' Read checked his watch. 'In fact, if you can give me forty-five minutes to wrap up something here, then my partner and I can be there ourselves to collect the documents from you.' Fairer formed a circle with his forefinger and thumb to approve the promise and Read nodded. 'Yes, DC Fairer and I can be there. ... Again, we do appreciate this. ... Yes, of course. We'll be with you shortly.'

'Finally, something we can work with,' Melanie said, turning to step toward her office.

'More than just the will,' Read said, disconnecting his call. 'Yarbury said that most of Ethan's belongings are going to the executor, bar a few personal items that look to be distributed among friends. The executor is a female name with a phoney address that Yarbury can't track down.'

'Spit out whatever the rest is, Read, we don't have time for smugness.'

Read's expression softened. 'Apparently when Ethan confirmed the details of his will, he also gave Yarbury a sealed envelope that wasn't to be opened by anyone named in the will.'

'No one named in the will? So, what, it was never meant to be opened?' Fairer asked.

'Or it was meant to be opened by someone who'd be waiting for a letter,' Carter suggested.

Melanie thought for a second, her eyebrows pulled together in confusion. But her expression relaxed as a realisation came to her.

'Unless he guessed it would be opened by us...'

27

I t had been nearly an hour since Read and Fairer had left the
station for the solicitor's office. Melanie had hoped they'd be
back by now, but given their laissez-faire attitude at the best of
times she wondered whether they'd stopped somewhere for
food along the way. Meanwhile, Morris was still battling through
one barrier after another on Ethan's computer – even with the
tech team lending her a hand – while Burton and Carter had
elected to jump between taking phone calls and watching CCTV
footage from Benny's café. Melanie had to admire the growing
determination her team had to find something on this case;
despite Read and Fairer taking their sweet time to catch-up with
the others. Although Melanie felt her judgement on them soften
when she watched Fairer step back into the office, and hold the
door open for his partner. Read followed seconds later, holding
a slim cardboard folder that was sealed in an evidence bag.

'Anyone order a letter from a dead guy?' Read said, causing
Burton to tut from behind her computer monitor.

'Anyone ever tell you that you're kind of a pig?'

Read looked as though he had genuinely considered the
question and said, 'Most days, actually.' He carried the docu-

ments over to the table in the centre of the room where Melanie was already pulling on latex gloves. 'Do we need forensics?'

'As long as we're gloved for the initial look, anything of use can be sent over to them once we've had a chance to read through things. Which means hands off to anyone who isn't wearing protection.' Melanie heard a snort from behind her. 'Grow up, Carter.'

'How did you even know it was me?'

Melanie passed a pair of gloves across to Burton. 'Apparently we're the only grown-ups.'

'Shocking,' Burton said, pulling on one glove then the other. 'Did the solicitor have any more pearls while you were over there?'

'He told us he's made copies of the will, but what we've got here is the original. The same applies to anything contained in that folder. The letter was sealed when Ethan gave it to him, so he really does have no idea what's in that,' Fairer said.

'But Ethan told him, definitively, it was a letter?' Melanie asked, unzipping the evidence bag.

'Yarbury told us that, yeah. Irwill said it was a letter, not to be opened by anyone named in the will, and apparently when Yarbury asked what he meant by that he said it would become obvious when the will was read.'

'But I'm guessing it hasn't become obvious at all?' Carter jumped in.

'I'm guessing he had a good reason for not mentioning this the first time we went to speak to him as well?' Melanie looked across to Fairer in time to catch him roll his eyes at the question. 'That good, I see.'

'He said it hadn't occurred to him until he really thought about things.'

'Which is a lie,' Read added.

Melanie laid the folder on the table and pulled out one sheet of paper at a time, inspecting it and sharing its contents with the team as she went. Yarbury had been right about one thing; the majority of Ethan's livelihood was going to one name in particular. Their mystery woman was set to inherit the victim's house, car and the contents of one bank account. Meanwhile, the rest of his monies had been split across his friends and one named charity.

'What charity?' Edd asked.

Burton sighed. 'Surely you mean, who's the woman?'

'You don't think the charity is important?' Edd asked, his tone jovial.

'Not as important as the woman who killed him, no,' Burton replied as she scanned the sheet Melanie had handed over to her. 'Dogs of Rescue, as you asked.'

'And Violet Linwood, not that you seem interested,' Melanie added. 'Did Yarbury say what he'd done to track the name down?' Melanie directed the question to Read and Fairer; it was the latter who answered.

'He said he had limited resources but he hadn't been able to match this woman to the address that's listed for her; the one that's on the first sheet.' He nodded toward the paper that Melanie was inspecting. 'He said he thought we'd have more resources than him, hence getting us involved.'

'Pillock should have got us involved from the off. Who wants to take this?' Melanie asked the group, the sheet pierced between her thumb and forefinger. 'I want to know who this woman is before end of play tomorrow.'

'Challenge accepted,' Read replied, picking up a loose glove from the table. 'Can we use Morris?'

'No, that's cheating,' Fairer answered. 'We've got this, boss.'

Melanie picked through the rest of the package until she found what they'd all been waiting for; the sealed envelope, addressed to no one in particular. She sucked in hard and held her breath as she lifted up the edge of the envelope's lip, easing the adhesive loose. The sheet of paper inside was as you'd expect; a bright white A4 page that, once she'd unfolded it, she could see was marked with a handwritten message in the centre. Melanie read it through to herself before releasing a laboured out breath and sharing the words with her team:

I don't know who will find this. Whoever you are, I imagine you'll be looking for her by now.
You won't find her, and I don't want you to. I know how it must look but it isn't what you all think it is; she isn't what people will make her.
I didn't tell anyone because it wasn't for anyone to know. But if you've found this then it must be out there by now. I wish there was a way for me to know how out there it is.
Please though, whoever you are. Stop looking.
E. Irwill.

There was a pall of silence over the room when Melanie finished reading. One team member looked to another but none of them ventured as far to speak. 'Thoughts?' Melanie pushed, but it was clear to her that all the group had for now was a daisy chain of shock threaded through them. She folded the paper down and set it on the table before clearing her throat. 'Okay, this is how it's going to go. Burton and Carter, you're going to carry on wading through phone calls and camera footage. If anything, and I mean bloody anything, comes up that looks or sounds like our woman, I want it followed up.'

'Yes, boss,' Burton said, already pulling off her gloves. Carter nodded his agreement.

'Read and Fairer, you're going to chase down this Violet Linwood. Start with the address. I don't care what Yarbury did or didn't find; people don't pull addresses out of nowhere, there's some significance, even if it gives us an area to rule out. Clear?'

'Got it,' the pair said, almost in unison.

'What are we doing with this?' Carter cast his eyes over the letter as he spoke.

'Do we have handwritten documents from Ethan's office still?' Melanie asked.

Burton gestured toward her desk. 'Piles of them. He was quite a record-keeper.'

'Right then.' Melanie snatched up the letter and stuffed it back into the envelope. 'I'm going to start by making sure our Ethan actually wrote the bloody thing.'

28

Carter stretched his mouth into an oversized yawn and unleashed a dramatic noise to accompany it. Burton side-eyed her partner but didn't give him the courtesy of a response; instead she clicked to the next video clip and leaned back in her chair, giving her back a needed stretch. The pair had been watching security footage since the previous afternoon and they were yet to spot anyone who looked like their mystery woman. But if what Benny's manager had told them was right, it could only be a matter of time before she appeared in their sightline.

'Come on, Burton, indulge me with some idle chit-chat. How's home?'

'Home? That's really what you want to talk about.'

'I'm not married now. I have to experience wedded bliss vicariously.'

Burton exhaled sharply. 'Bliss is a stretch. How's your home?'

'Hard pass on that line of questioning then, eh?' Carter pushed but when Burton didn't respond he changed tactics. 'Trish doesn't want me to have shared custody.'

Burton shot Carter a raised eyebrow. 'Why the hell not?'

'She says I'm not around enough.'

'That's rich. Has she been on any midweek dates recently?' Burton asked as something on-screen caught her eye. 'Wait a second, wait, hit pause there.'

Carter leaned forward to hit pause and the screen stuttered to a stop over the image of a young woman. She bore an uncanny resemblance to the picture that was pieced together by their sketch artist, but there was also something different about this woman that took a second for either officer to place.

'Is her hair shorter?' Burton asked, as she tipped her head to one side.

'Her hair is shorter, and those glasses are different.'

Burton clicked her fingers. 'Okay, so, what are we thinking? Is she or isn't she?'

'I don't know, Burton, I'm not convinced. She's just...' he trailed off and started to click through the frames of the video that followed this initial sighting, before eventually letting the footage run again at its normal speed.

'Just what?'

'She could be anyone, couldn't she? I'm just not convinced that this woman is even distinct enough for us to find. She's not pretty, she's not distinctive, she's not–'

Burton leaned across her partner to reach for the pause button. 'She's meeting Ethan Irwill though.'

Carter looked back down at the screen and there the woman was, plain as day, sitting at a table with their victim. The pair had leaned in as though engaging in quiet conversation, but from the camera angle it was easy to spot the comfort of their expressions towards each other.

'We need printouts of this. Let's skip back to when the woman is on her own,' Carter ordered, and Burton began to click back through the frames. 'I think it might be worth paying our Ian Tatham a visit this afternoon, don't you?'

~

Melanie looked along the walls of Hilda Addair's office. The woman was a celebrated academic, author and, most importantly, a forensic linguist. Melanie had heard of her before in passing but she'd never had reason to involve such an expert on one of her own cases – until this latest reveal. Photocopies of the letter and the handwriting sample that Melanie pulled from Ethan's personal belongings lay in the police officer's lap, a thin sheath of plastic protecting both items. She teased the corner of one plastic wallet, pinching the layers between her thumb and forefinger until their quiet crackle occupied the room. She wasn't sure how long she'd been waiting, but she knew she was lucky to have made it into Addair's office at all at such short notice. The woman who had seen her in had explained this was special treatment – 'She's a fan of your work, you know?' – and Melanie had been grateful for the small mercy, despite not fully understanding it.

'DI Melanie Watton, I can only apologise for the delay.'

Melanie heard the voice before she saw the woman. But when Melanie made eye contact with the academic, she could see that the booming Scottish voice fit her appearance entirely. Addair's hair was a fierce red, complemented by the blush in her cheeks – *from rushing from one meeting to another*, Melanie wondered – and her build was what Melanie's mother would refer to as sturdy.

'Students galore, I just can't bloody rid myself of them.' She extended a hand as she spoke and, once Melanie had reciprocated the gesture, Addair moved around to the opposite side of the desk and dropped herself heavily into her chair. 'I'm delighted to hear from you, DI Watton, I must say. The high school case you worked last year had me rapt.'

Melanie wished she could take the remark as a compliment.

But she at least managed to swallow down her discomfort. 'Well, I think it certainly had a lot of people interested.'

'Teenagers,' Addair said, while appearing to look for something on her desk. 'They're some of the most dangerous animals we're breeding these days, don't you think?'

'I don't know about that, Dr Addair. In my line of work, you see monsters of all ages.'

Addair stopped her searching then and met Melanie's gaze. 'Which is precisely why I was so happy to hear that I could be of some use to you.' She rested her forearms on the desk and leaned in closer to Melanie to ask, 'Have you brought me a monster then, DI Watton?'

The tone would have been flirtatious had the question not been another uncomfortable one from the academic. Melanie responded by lifting the sheets from her lap and setting them down in front of the woman's stare. 'We have two handwriting samples and I need to know if there's a way of working out whether both were written by the same person.'

'But of course there is.' Addair leaned back and reached for a pair of glasses to the left of her. She swapped them for the pair she was wearing before picking up the first handwriting sample; a collection of telephone notes that Ethan had left lying on his study desk. 'So, is this the victim or the perpetrator?' The query was met with silence, so the doctor looked up from her work to Melanie. 'You must think I'm awfully gruesome.'

Melanie laughed to soften the accusation, despite the accuracy of it. 'I think people who don't work with these things every day can find them a little more interesting than those of us who do. I don't know that that's especially gruesome.'

Addair felt around her desk to find a small magnifying loupe that she used against the sheet of writing. She held the glass over one point, then another, reading through what looked to Melanie like a random sample of words – although she guessed there must be more to it. Satisfied with whatever she had found in this first sample, Addair moved to repeat the process with the second text; the letter that had been held by Ethan's solicitor. The doctor scanned the letter before looking back at Melanie.

'Victim then?' she said, a smirk appearing. Before Melanie could open her mouth, Addair shook her head lightly. 'Worry not, detective, I'm excellent at keeping secrets.' She winked at Melanie before looking back at the paper.

Addair spent ten minutes going from one sheet of paper to the other and back again. Midway through this process, Melanie went back to inspecting the walls around the office. Each one boasted a new certificate, a new expert knowledge in one thing or another. Melanie had to admit she was impressed with the doctor's professional qualifications and her obvious expertise; even if the woman did appear a touch over-friendly.

'There's more that I can do,' Addair started, catching Melanie's attention. 'Full and proper analyses that we can perform, if we had a little more time, and if they weren't such confidential texts, of course.' She handed them both back to Melanie but thought for a second longer before announcing, 'In my professional opinion, they're both written by the same person. Like I said, there are more tests if you want to be completely certain, but I'd bet good money on it as it stands. They use the same drops in letters, the same cursive between letters. It would be enough to convince a jury, I should think. If you needed it to, that is.' Her tone moved from professional to flirtatious again in the final words, but Melanie didn't quite mind as much now.

'So, the full letter, you don't think it's a forgery?'

Addair shook her head. 'I definitely don't. They were written by the same person. But whether that person had a gun to their head when the letter was written, that I can't say.'

No, Melanie thought, *no, a gun isn't our woman's style.*

29

Burton and Carter had left a note on Melanie's desk to let her know they were chasing up a lead. *Information on what the lead was would have been worthwhile*, Melanie thought, but she trusted them both to make their own judgement calls at this point. She filed away the letter and the handwriting sample, and she stacked Hilda's business card on top of the growing pile of them on her desk. The number of times she'd heard, 'Call me if I can help,' from too-eager academics looking for public exposure was eye-watering. Although Melanie couldn't stifle the feeling that Hilda's intentions hadn't been entirely career-based.

The shadow of someone walking past her open doorway caught Melanie's attention and she looked up in time to catch Read and Fairer grabbing their jackets.

'Do we have any news on Violet?' she said, walking out into the open space.

'Maybe. We've got a Violet who lived in the address area until recently, but a different last name,' Fairer replied.

'We thought it was worth a poke around though,' Read added.

Melanie agreed. 'Let me know if anything comes up, okay?'

Once the office door had closed shut behind the pair of them, Melanie crossed the room to Morris. She was clicking through what looked to be lines of code; beyond that, Melanie couldn't identify much that was happening. She waited until the series of clicks and taps had slowed down before letting out a gentle cough.

Morris jumped before she turned. 'I'm sorry, boss, I was... involved.' She laughed.

'May I?' Melanie tapped the back of the empty chair sitting alongside Morris' desk and when the DC gestured for her to take it, she sat down. 'Can we have a talk about something that might be stupid?'

'I doubt it will be stupid.'

'You haven't heard the request yet, and you know a lot more about these godforsaken things than I do.' Melanie knocked the side of Morris' computer monitor. 'I was wondering if there's a way for us to get back onto the dark web, maybe using Ethan's login details, so we can get easier access to his chats.'

Morris frowned. 'Is that the stupid thing?'

'No, this next part is. Is there any way that we can use Ethan's access on there to somehow search for the Domdomdom username, to see when that account was last active in any of the forums that we know she likes to use?'

'Sure there is, but it might take some searching. Plus we scoped out as much as we could the last time we logged in through Ethan's account.'

'But she's gone quiet, Morris, and that makes me nervous. If she's still using these forums, which she may well be, then there could be another victim on her radar already.' Morris nodded her understanding and turned to scribble something on a pad of Post-its positioned underneath her monitor. Melanie waited for her to finish. 'Okay, so what are you working on the moment?'

Morris back-clicked out of the coded screen that had

hovered in the background and replaced it with what Melanie could recognise as a locked document. Along the centre of the screen there was a slim grey bar that showed an ever-changing series of numbers. The progress of the bar was, Melanie estimated, around three quarters of the way through whatever was being scanned. As the officers watched, the bar alternated between hardly noticeable movements and sudden jerks along the screen.

'I might be looking for a door that doesn't exist,' Morris started, and turned to face Melanie. 'But I've copied Ethan's laptop over onto my own desktop to play around with these documents some more. I thought, given that we've got all of his other passwords now, we might be able to use a password scrambler to work out the last two passwords that we need for these locked documents.'

'So, you think you can crack them open?'

'I'm hoping that I can. Using the passwords we've got, the software can piece together possible revisions of each password to scan the documents for their actual password. I've managed to tweak the software to include some key words in the search as well, things we've picked up as important to the victim, basic stuff really. As each possibility is created by the scrambler, the software checks it against the document itself and if it doesn't work then it moves on to the next revision, you see?'

Melanie hesitated. 'I think I see enough to get your meaning, yes.'

'I can leave that going in the background if you want me to get started on the dark web?' Before Melanie could respond, Morris turned back to the computer and pulled up a window that Melanie recognised all too quickly as the dark web login page. 'It would be easier if we could just scan the whole software for signs of the name but no such luck. I can pull up the forums we found her on last time though. I don't know what Dumb and

Dumber are working on at the moment, but I can leave instructions for them to take a forum each when they get back as well if you like?' When Melanie didn't respond, Morris turned to her. Melanie had a cocked eyebrow and a smirk. 'What did I do?'

'Dumb and dumber?'

'I mean, DCs Read and Fairer.' Morris flushed. 'I'm sorry, boss.'

'Is that what you call them?'

Morris hesitated. 'Is that not what you call them?'

The computer behind Morris chirped an announcement for something, pulling back her attention. She clicked through a series of messages before hovering the cursor over an *Open* button that had appeared on the screen. 'This can't be it,' she said, before clicking her mouse. The white screen of a word document unfolded, and Morris leaned back in her chair as though giving the software room to spread its limbs.

'Is this what I think it is?' Melanie asked, leaning in next to Morris so she could watch the document stir into life.

A string of characters unfolded in a way that Melanie had never seen a document load before. She wondered whether it was a by-product of the hi-tech security, but from the look on Morris' face she hadn't seen anything of the sort before either. The paragraphs, sentences, words appeared to load in a patchwork order which meant that nearly a whole minute had passed before the document appeared – but it still wasn't quite fully formed. Morris adjusted the size quality to get as much as she could on the screen at once. Despite the missing information, it became clear all too quickly what the pair were looking at.

They took their time scanning the information before Morris asked, 'Is that even legal? Like, is this a real thing?'

Melanie shook her head in slow motion, her eyes fixed to the screen.

'I've honestly got no idea. I've never come across anything like this before.'

Every time Melanie reached the bottom of the page, she felt compelled to shift her eyes upward and start afresh. On each read through a new set of words jumped out but after the fourth scan she was sure she'd got everything she was going to get without a solicitor, or a barrister, being present. She pulled a scrap of paper and a pen from Morris' desk to note down the key terms; the ones she'd need to take to Archer. Melanie flitted between document and paper until the small sheet was covered in her own handwriting, the words listed in bullet-point form.

- Of sound mind
- Free will
- Affairs in order
- Killed on demand.

30

Carter kept the phone pressed to his ear but shook his head at Burton; no, Melanie hadn't answered. 'Hi, boss, it's me and Burton here. Look, we got Ethan on camera earlier today with a woman matching the description that Tatham gave us. We've paid the man himself an impromptu visit and he's said it definitely is the woman who came to see him and...' Carter pulled the phone away and gave it a hard stare. 'Arses.'

'What?'

'I think it must have timed out.'

Burton sighed. 'You need to be more concise.'

Carter hit the green icon next to Melanie's name and placed the phone back at his ear. 'Me again, bloody voicemails. It's definitely the woman who came to see him, in case you didn't get that. Burton and I are about to start casing coffee shops around the centre. We thought if she's not going to her old haunt...' Carter repeated the same gesture of staring at the phone before dropping the handset into his back pocket. 'Fuck it, I'm not ringing again.'

'Why do you think she isn't answering?' Burton asked, opening the passenger door to their shared vehicle.

'Maybe there's a lead at the station?'

Both officers climbed into the car and as Carter buckled in Burton pulled her phone from her jacket pocket. She opened a fresh web page and typed in *coffee shops local to me.* She set the phone on her leg as she did up her seat belt and waited for the information to load.

'Where do you want to start?' she asked, when the list appeared.

Carter craned over to take a look at the screen. 'There are loads of them, Chris.'

'Yep, coffee shops are a basic need nowadays.'

'Oh sure, like air and water I hear,' Carter said, flicking on the indicator and checking his blind spot. 'Go from the top of the list and we'll just see how far we get. Plan?'

'Papa's, on New Street.'

Carter and Burton were four coffee shops through their list when they pushed through the double doors of Lily's; home to the best halloumi sandwich in town, according to the A-board that stood outside the shop.

'The fact that that's their boast tells me everything I need to know about this place,' Carter said, coming to a stop alongside Burton in the queue. There were only one or two people waiting to be served, so the pair opted to wait in line.

'Can we talk to the manager, please?' Carter said, coming to a stop at the front of the line. He flashed his ID badge and watched a look of unease spread across the face of the young woman behind the counter. *That always does the trick*, he thought. 'It's quite important,' he added, when she didn't show signs of moving. But she scurried from behind the counter without a word then and rushed somewhere behind the two officers. When Carter and Burton turned to track her, they saw her talking hurriedly to a man who was sitting at a corner table in the café.

'You're meaner than you need to be sometimes, you know that,' Burton said as she and her partner turned to face the counter space again.

Carter let out a curt laugh. 'Says you.'

'He'll be a minute.' The young woman resumed her stance behind the counter, and she seemed much calmer than she had a moment before. Carter noticed a hint of something non-native about her accent, and with some guilt he wondered whether that might account for her initial nervousness towards them.

'Thanks, that's great.'

'How can I be of service to you today?' The chirpy voice came from behind them seconds later, pulling their attention round. The man wore a managerial smile. *He's accustomed to wearing a game face*, Carter thought.

'I'm DS Carter, this is my partner DC Burton. We wondered whether we might have a quick chat with you, somewhere quieter?' Carter said, nodding to the queue that was forming behind them.

'Of course, my workspace is just here.' He turned and wandered back toward the table for two he'd occupied when the officers walked in. He pulled up an extra seat and resumed the same position, back in front of his laptop. 'I find it so much easier working out here than in the back office,' he added, his smile loosening into something more natural. He waited for both officers to take a seat before he asked, 'What is it I can help you with?'

'We're actually trying to track down someone, who we suspect might be involved in an ongoing investigation,' Burton started while Carter manoeuvred the photograph from his inside jacket pocket. 'If you could take a look at this image and let us know whether the face rings a bell at all, it'd be really helpful to us.'

The man took the photograph but held eye contact with Burton. 'Hey, this isn't anything to do with that murder on the television, is it?'

Carter had to hold back from rolling his eyes at the man's obvious excitement. 'Nothing quite so glamorous, I'm afraid. If you could just let us know whether you recognise the woman pictured here...' Carter trailed off when the man looked down to follow instructions. Carter flashed a quick unimpressed face at Burton who matched his expression.

'Sure, she's recently started coming in here.'

Carter's head snapped toward the man. 'You're sure of that?'

'Completely. I'm here most days and I'd say I see her, I don't know, a couple of times a week at least.' He looked at the image again. 'It's definitely her. She's quiet though, you know, tends to keep herself to herself.'

I'll bet she does, Carter thought. 'Has she been in here with anyone, can you remember?'

The man thought for a moment and took another look at the image, as though trying to jog a memory. 'No one that I can think of, no. She comes in, orders her drink, sets up her laptop and that's it. We tab her drinks for a few hours and then she pays and leaves.'

'Does she bring her laptop in every time?' Burton asked.

'Yep, every time. I asked whether she was working once and she sort of, I don't know, grunted as a reply.' He laughed lightly. 'She's pretty engrossed in whatever work she brings here, that's all I can tell you. I'm sure she's a nice woman when you get to know her though.' He laughed again and Carter's stomach rolled over.

'You said she's here often, can you remember when exactly you last saw her?'

'Yesterday.'

'You seem pretty sure about that,' Burton replied.

'Completely sure. There was a power cut that took out the whole street yesterday afternoon. We lost so much produce during those hours, it was ridiculous.'

'I'm sorry, why does that make you so sure...'

'Oh!' he added, as though realising his explanation was an incomplete one. 'It took out our internet for most of the afternoon. The woman, she waited around half an hour or so, I guess to see whether it was coming back on, then she came to ask me whether I could tell her when it'd be coming back on.' He shrugged. 'She seemed pretty put out by the whole thing and when I said we didn't know much, she settled her tab, grabbed her computer and left.'

Carter and Burton exchanged a quick look before the DS continued. 'This has been really helpful, sir, thank you so much for giving up some of your time today.' Carter stood and Burton followed suit, leaving the manager – who looked a touch disappointed – sitting at his table-turned-desk alone.

'Should I call if she comes in again?'

'I shouldn't think there's a need for that. Having a rough idea of her usual haunts will be help enough for us. Thank you again, truly.' Carted rushed through his goodbye and followed Burton, who was already halfway through the door of the shop.

'If she was here yesterday, online here as recently as yesterday, presumably she was writing as Domdomdom as recently as yesterday too,' Burton said, her words heavy with breath as she and Carter power-walked back towards the car.

'Even better, Burton. If she was online as Domdomdom in that shop yesterday, we've got a perfect spot for a stake-out...'

31

Melanie licked her finger and thumb to separate one piece of paper from the next. She flicked through handouts, checking there were enough sheets for one copy apiece, before calling together the attention of her team. Everyone sat in front of her, a mixture of tired eyes and excited stares, and Melanie imagined she must look much the same. Morris had talked her through finding Domdomdom on the dark web chat forums and, although Melanie understood that it would take a while – and a lot of manpower – to wade through the sheer amount of content, she couldn't resist making a start on research at least, if only to understand more about this part of the internet. When her alarm had gone off for this early meeting, she'd instantly regretted getting sucked into the black hole of the internet – with nothing to show for it, either. But at least she'd got the extracts from the contract that Morris had found and, after a day or two of silence from much of her team, she expected them to have their own breakthroughs too.

'Who's going first?' she asked the room, and the officers looked between themselves.

'Burton and I are going last because we've got the best thing,' Carter announced.

Morris snorted. 'I doubt it.'

'We'll go,' Fairer said, his tone deflated in comparison to his colleagues'. 'We've got bugger all, essentially. Apparently Violet is in the wind as well as any one woman can be. We asked around the area that the address is rooted in, people remember a Violet-something and that's as specific as they can be. We found a house that was previously registered to, and inhabited by, a Violet Munston, but that's as close to her name as we can get, and it's been a good twelve months since anyone can place her on the street anyway.'

'I thought she'd been registered there until recently?' Melanie asked.

Read shrugged. 'So did we, boss, according to everything that we could find online too. But there was a discrepancy between when she vacated the house and when the house changed ownership; human error somewhere down the line.'

Melanie was disappointed but she tried not to let it show. The last thing she needed was a dip in team morale. 'Well, at least you've ruled something out and we've got another Violet to run-through the system. Have you had a look for this other Violet yet?'

'That's today's job,' Read replied.

'Okay, good. Carter, you're up.'

'Can't Morris go next?'

'No, because she and I have got the best thing,' Melanie said, giving Morris a playful wink. There was a soft, 'Oooh,' that echoed around the room from Read, Fairer and Burton.

'Do you want something for that burn or are you going to let the air get to it?' Morris asked, leaning over her chair to get a look at Carter.

'Hey, don't forget who your superior officer is,' Carter snapped.

'Likewise.' Melanie's tone was flat, and it silenced the room. She didn't mind a gentle joke to lift spirits, but they needed to keep their focus as well. 'Burton, fill us all in, would you?'

'Carter and I managed to find our mystery woman. We had the photo sketch to go from, obviously, and we were watching the security footage from Benny's when, would you believe it, not only does a woman matching the sketch come wandering in but Ethan Irwill eventually joins her. We took a still of the woman to Tatham to see if he could identify her and he did; he seemed pretty certain about it as well. From there we started going to the cafés in the town to see whether anyone else might recognise the woman, now we've got an actual photo of her.'

'By the by, do you know how many cafés and coffee shops there are in town?' Carter added before completing the details of their breakthrough.

Melanie felt a physical ease of tension in her stomach. 'This is really good work, both of you. I want someone on that coffee shop every hour they're open. Do you know what their hours are?'

'Eight in the morning until seven at night,' Burton answered.

Melanie checked her watch. 'Okay, as soon as this is over, are you two happy to take the first shift?' She waited for a nod from Carter and Burton in turn. 'Brilliant. We'll draw up a rota from here on out until we find her, which shouldn't take long if she's visiting that often. That everything?'

'Everything from us,' Carter said.

'Which brings us on to this then,' Melanie said as she pulled the first sheet of paper from her small pile and handed it to Morris. She repeated the gesture until everyone was holding a copy of the contract, or rather, as much of the contract as Morris had been able to find, and she gave her team the time to read over the details. When their shocked expressions lifted one by one, she knew they'd had enough time. 'Morris has managed to crack into one of two locked documents on Ethan's computer; obviously, this is the one that we have access to. Thanks to the jiggery-pokery on the laptop, we can't access the whole thing yet. But there's obviously enough here for us to draw conclusions. Morris, could you?' Melanie asked, giving Morris her cue to pull the document up on the interactive whiteboard for ease of access. 'You'll see from this that the person who is to be signing the document – I think it's a fair assumption that it was intended for Ethan – is claiming they're of sound mind and in a proper state to be entering into an agreement like this.'

'Can you be of sound mind if you're agreeing to something like this?' Burton asked.

'Well, that'll be a question for the prosecution and defence to thrash out, I imagine. We can also see from this that the person signing it claims to have their affairs in order, which, we can assume, is why Ethan decided to arrange for a will out of nowhere despite not needing one before. 'Killed on demand' in the final phrase is causing Archer some concern, although I think the meaning of it is fairly clear given the context of Ethan's death.'

'So, Archer has seen this?' Carter asked.

'She has, she's steaming at the ears, and she's trying to answer the question that's no doubt on everyone's lips, is this agreement actually binding?'

'Oh, come on,' Read said. 'Surely it can't be? Who agrees to be killed?'

'It's happened though, hasn't it? In other countries?' Morris asked the room.

'Not quite like this, I don't think,' Burton replied, and she was right, Melanie thought. From her rushed research before presenting this document to her superior, she couldn't find a case that was exactly like this one – but she could find ones that were similar.

'There are cases that are similar to this where people have agreed to be killed, yes,' Melanie clarified. 'But it's the contract that's likely to complicate matters.'

'What, just because he put it in writing?' Carter asked.

'No, because he put it in a legal document,' Morris replied.

'Legal or not, there are a lot of questions to be answered about what difference this actually makes to the case, particularly given the parts of the deal that we don't have access to yet. But Archer is looking to answer these questions. Nevertheless, we need to remain aware of this complication going forward,' Melanie said, trying to draw their chatter to a conclusion. 'Alongside this, Morris and I have also talked about the possibility of tracking down Domdomdom through her chatroom and forum use. It turns out it's a bigger job than I thought given that we can't isolate one fetish, sex-thing, whatever forum from another, so it's a case of reading a lot of dark material and hoping for a name, if anyone especially fancies it.'

Burton raised a hand. 'I'm not offering, but the chap who Carter and I spoke to at the coffee shop, he said the woman had been in the day before, which makes it the day before yesterday now. If she's going there to use their internet, maybe it's for the dark web stuff? I don't know whether that scales down the search,' she said, directing the query at Morris.

Morris thought for a second. 'There might be a way to use that, actually.'

'Brilliant. Carter and Burton, you take the coffee shop. Fairer, you can team up with Morris for the morning to help with the dark web searches and Read, you can take Violet on your own, unless something crops up. Fair deal?' There was a noise of general agreement from the team before Melanie set them free about their tasks. She would have happily traded with any of them when she looked at the clock and noted the time. There were only thirty minutes of preparation before her catch-up meeting with Archer, and with that contract now clogging up the arteries of the case, Melanie wasn't expecting anything good.

32

Straightandnarrow:

Aren't you worried that you'll get caught

Domdomdom:

I haven't been so far

Saltandpeppered:

I'm calling bullsh!t

I don't believe for a second that you've done this

More than once as well

Domdomdom:

Only one way to find out if I'm telling the truth…

Straightandnarrow:

You're looking for someone new then?

Domdomdom:

Always

Straightandnarrow:

How long has it been since you last killed someone?

…

Are you still there?
Domdomdom:
Killing someone makes it sound like something
it isn't
Stringmealong/up:
So what do you call it then?
Domdomdom:
Snuff
Straightandnarrow:
So: how long is it since you last snuffed
someone?
Domdomdom:
A few weeks
Straightandnarrow:
Can you tell me about it?
We can talk in private if you want
Too soon?

'She didn't come back online after that, but Fairer left her a private message as part of this forum. We should be able to see when she reads it,' Morris said, closing down the interactive screen. She returned to her seat to await judgement.

Melanie rubbed at her forehead. 'Which one of you thought this was a good idea?'

Fairer glanced over at Morris and said, 'Both of us, to be honest.'

'We found her hanging around in other rooms, fetish rooms, where she's had the odd exchange with people, but nothing seemed to be coming from any of it. So, we thought if we at least gave her some bait to work with–'

'Fairer isn't bait,' Melanie cut across her junior. 'He's your bloody colleague.'

'Boss, if I can cut in?' Carter asked, and Melanie encouraged him to take over. 'I think what DI Watton is trying to say here is that the problem isn't what you did.'

'Carter...' Melanie cautioned.

'It's more the fact that you did it without considering the rest of the investigation, and the team. This should have been a decision that DI Watton or, at the very least, I was involved in making. You can't go off half-cocked with what you think is a good idea without talking to other people about it first. That much is clear, surely?'

Morris answered for the pair of them, 'We appreciate that now, yes, and we're both sorry for the indiscretion, DI Watton.'

Melanie noted the fact that the apology had extended past Carter and come directly to her. She didn't know whether that made Morris a kiss-ass or a clever DC; she suspected it might be a mixture of both. Either way, the reprimand was over with and she'd managed to sidestep the duty herself, so that was something to be grateful for.

'Now that the official stuff is out the way,' Melanie said, taking back the baton of conversation. 'I do actually think this was a good idea, and it's another way we can try to lure this woman out into the open, which is obviously our main goal at this point.'

'What irks me is the time of these messages. You were doing this when, eight last night?' Carter asked.

'Eight thirty through until around nine, which is when she dropped out,' Fairer replied.

'Burton and I were on that coffee shop until they shut up shop for the evening.'

'Okay, so we've got a second location to find,' Melanie replied.

'Might she be at home?' Fairer added.

Morris thought for a moment. 'If she's smart, she could be

doing this from home and using an IP scrambler, which would make it harder to isolate her location.'

'But if she's doing that then why would she need the coffee shop at all?' Carter asked.

'Maybe she's casing out the coffee shop as a meeting place, for when and if someone bites. That way she has a place she's already familiar with, but she can keep up her conversations while she's at it,' Melanie said, and a murmur of agreement followed. 'Fairer, you and Read are meant to be teaming up for coffee watch today, and it looks to me like you've had little enough contact with the woman for someone to step in and talk in your place if she appears again, so you're off this for now. Morris, I want printouts of everything she's said in the other forums you've found.'

'But there's nothing about the snuff films in there.'

'I don't care. I want to know how she talks, who she's talking to, where she's going, the lot of it. Anything that can help is worth looking into right now.'

Melanie dismissed the two junior officers to go about their daily business. When it was just her and Carter left in the room, she sank against the back of her chair, ran a hand through her hair and unleashed a sigh that soon became a moan.

'That bad?' Carter asked, sitting down opposite her.

'I don't know what more we can be doing, other than waiting around for the woman to kill someone else.'

'She prefers you not to use the word "kill", actually.'

From Carter's tone Melanie could tell he was trying to be light-hearted, but she couldn't raise a smile. 'I'm serious, Edd. We don't have forensics, we don't have a witness, we barely even have a crime scene, and the only strong piece of evidence we've managed to pull could, in theory, exonerate her from the entire thing.'

'Archer thinks that the contract will hold?'

'It shouldn't, and the legals she's consulted on it think it won't, but there's no way to guarantee a good solicitor won't try to give it weight. In fact, I'd be more surprised if one didn't.'

'So, what happens then? The good guys fight to get the contract thrown out?'

Melanie let out a hard exhale. 'They will, assuming we ever bloody catch her.'

33

Carter walked into the open office carrying four cups of takeaway coffee precariously wedged into a cardboard container. He dropped a cup off at Morris' desk without saying a word to disturb the detective. Burton was next along the line of workers. It had been two days since the coffee shop stake-out had started and they were yet to find a break in the case for their mystery woman. But Carter had to admit that shoving Read and Fairer on watch duty had its perks; a quiet office being one of them. He set a flat white next to Burton who had her head buried in paperwork. It had been hours since she'd spoken to anyone.

'Am I allowed to ask?' Carter said, and Burton held up her right index finger. Carter didn't know whether that was a 'No,' or a 'Wait one minute.' When the seconds rolled by without another comment from his partner, he decided it must be the former and he continued his rounds; the next stop was Melanie's office. The door was shut but Carter hoped an interruption for caffeine would be a welcome one. He gave one firm tap with his knuckles and waited.

'Come in.'

Carter pushed the door open and removed an Americano from the cardboard tray. He held it out in front of him, at a safe distance, he thought.

'Carter, I don't know that I've ever been gladder to see you.' Melanie beckoned him toward her and took the coffee from him as soon as she could reach it.

'I don't know that that's a compliment, boss, but you're welcome.'

'How's everything out there?'

Carter puffed. 'Morris has been looking at what I'd guess is computer code for most of the morning, and Burton went off on a hunch three hours ago and hasn't spoken to me since.'

'What hunch?' Melanie removed the lid from her drink and blew hard against the liquid, sending a small ripple across the surface.

'Your guess is as good as mine. I asked whether I was allowed to ask and she didn't–'

Burton stormed in, forcing a stop to Carter's sentence. She slammed a sheet of paper down on the mess of Melanie's desk with such a force that she jerked back in her seat, spilling her coffee over the lip of its cup.

'I bloody knew it,' Burton announced.

Melanie caught the stray drops of liquid before they could drip onto her trousers. 'Burton, I don't have spare trousers, just FYI.'

'Boss, I bloody knew I'd seen the name before,' Burton said, tapping the paper.

'What name?' Carter asked.

'Violet Munston, right? A spin-off from Violent Linwood? The more I heard the chaps talking about it, the more I became convinced I'd come across the name before, I just couldn't place where. The only place I thought I might have spotted it was somewhere in Ethan's things, when we went through them for his work details.'

Melanie picked up the sheet to look it over. 'And you found?'

'A contract between them.'

'Not the contract we found on the computer?'

'No, an actual contract where Violet contacted Ethan about some content development work for a website she was putting together.'

'What kind of website?' Carter asked, crossing the room to stand behind Melanie. He looked over his boss' shoulder to read the details for himself.

'A completely fictional one. I've looked up the site that he was hired to work on and there's no such domain name. I've asked Morris to check through Ethan's emails again. I don't see how they negotiated a contract without ever having met before, but their dark web exchanges make it sound like they didn't know each other. Unless that was part of the experience? Pretending to be strangers?'

'For what it's worth,' Morris said, coming to stand in the doorway. 'I've found a handful of emails on Ethan's laptop. The email address doesn't involve our suspect Violet, but there's a VLMunston@Munstonworks.com who contacted Ethan via his website some months back.'

'How many months are we talking?' Melanie asked.

'Eight.'

'Before they even met online,' Carter said, scanning the contract again. 'Which fits with this date too. But I don't get it. They worked together but they never met, is that what we're thinking here?'

Morris held up one of the sheets to read from. 'It's been a real pleasure to work with a client who knows what they want. Maybe next time we can work face to face. All the best.' She dropped the sheet. 'That's the last email I can find from Ethan to that email address, and Violet emailed back with something similar. Their first exchange is a neutral one, where she provides details of the job and he gives her a quote. There's nothing untoward in anything that I've skimmed through so far, but I can search for keywords now we've got somewhere new to look for them.'

'Okay, outside.' Melanie stood from her desk and trailed out of the room with the detectives following behind her. She grabbed a marker pen and wrote the date of the contract in one corner of an empty whiteboard, and the date of Ethan's murder in the other. 'Violet contacts Ethan to arrange for work on a website that doesn't exist. They exchange emails for a while, let's work on the assumption that they're professional and non-sexual until we have cause to think otherwise. They work together without meeting, and it doesn't strike Ethan as odd?'

'I don't think it would. Technology-based work can be done remotely these days and someone of Ethan's level would have been comfortable with that, I think,' Morris explained.

'Okay, it doesn't strike Ethan as odd. Then, by chance, they meet in a dark web forum some months later, where neither of them had usernames that identified them to each other?' Melanie wrote out a rough timeline across the board as she spoke. 'I don't buy it. I don't buy that they didn't know they were talking to each other at this point.'

'There has to be a link somewhere though,' Burton said, studying the board. 'Maybe Violet knew but Ethan didn't?'

'She must have found out what Ethan was into somehow and used the dark web as a means of making contact, rather than using this work persona. But why go to that kind of trouble?' Melanie said.

Carter looked at the span of details in front of them. The only thing that could make any sense to him now was that there must be another person involved; someone who knew that

Ethan was into unconventional sex play, and someone who would have let that slip to Violet.

'What if we talk to Fin Gallagher and Scott Kerrick again?' Carter suggested. 'Someone has put Violet onto Ethan. They must have done, because there's a missing link here and the only thing that makes sense is for it to be another person.'

'You think they were in on it somehow?' Melanie asked, her tone sceptical.

'No, I think Violet got lucky in talking to one of them and they put her onto their sometimes-a-bit-kinky friend,' Carter clarified.

'And she used the work as a way of... what?' Burton asked.

'Oh, Christ.' Morris stepped back from their circle and retreated to her desk. She crouched over her monitor and keyed in a few different commands to set the computer searching for something. 'She might have been using their online talks to access his laptop remotely,' she said, turning back to the group. 'I've got a copy of all of the software that was on Ethan's computer so if that's the case then we'll know in a few seconds.'

'Working theory,' Carter said, taking the board pen from Melanie. He added in details as he spoke. 'Violet is looking for a new man in her life and she gets lucky by meeting someone, let's not name names, who happens to know Ethan. It comes up in conversation, drunk conversation, that person X isn't especially interested in the kinky stuff, but they've got a friend who is.'

'Carter, come on. I think it's a stretch to think a bloke would share those details...' Melanie started but Carter raised his eyebrow to stop her. 'Good God. Right, okay, continue.'

'Violet wants to know exactly how kinky we're talking, so she contacts Ethan. Hypothetically, she has a few chats with him via email and uses this to send over some sort of virus that can access his computer somehow. She has a good poke around to see whether Ethan is as kinky as she needs him to be and hey presto, she's got her next person. When they arrange for the will, it's just a coincidence that she shares a first name with a former client, and from what we've seen Ethan had plenty of clients anyway. Violet Munston is long forgotten by the time Violet Linwood takes Ethan's life. Thoughts?'

Burton scanned the details on the board before answering. 'It's far-fetched.' As though realising how blunt her assessment sounded, she turned to Melanie and added, 'Don't you think it's a little far-fetched?'

'I think he might be right,' Morris announced. She stood doubled-over in front of her monitor, clicking from one thing to another. Carter was on the cusp of speeding her along; he couldn't stand the tension, and he was desperate to know whether this was a workable theory for them now. Morris stood and faced the group. 'He's right. There's old software on here that someone has tried to scrub at some point; I don't know how I didn't spot it before. She wouldn't have had remote access or anything quite so advanced, but she would have been able to see what software Ethan relied on, including the dark web download that ran the forums.'

'So, she actually watched him? This wasn't just a chance encounter?' Burton asked.

'We need to haul in Ethan's friends, like Carter suggested. There must be something more to find there. I want Fin and Scott in before the day is out,' Melanie said, giving the order to no one in particular. She lingered in front of the board for a second longer, her head shifting as she looked from one point to the next.

'What are you thinking, boss?' Carter asked, coming to stand alongside her.

'I'm thinking Violet is a much better killer than we'd given her credit for.' She turned to face Carter. 'But I'm also thinking we might have found her first mistake.'

34

Fairer and Read were on desk duty. Following their most recent stint stationed outside the coffee shop, Melanie had quickly filled them in on the latest developments before assigning them their daily duties. 'We need to follow any paper trails we can; anything that involves Violet, Munston or otherwise, we need to track down everything,' Melanie had ordered within ten minutes of the pair arriving at their desks, and they'd been buried under paperwork, digital and physical, since then. Morris was still wading through the contents of Ethan's laptop, her iPhone earplugs tucked in to shut out the noise of her colleagues.

'I swear to God, I don't know what she finds to do on those things,' Read said.

Fairer clicked through a PDF. 'Which is why she's the tech expert and you're not.'

'I could be.'

'But you're not.'

'Yeah, but–'

Fairer pushed back from his desk to bring his expression level with that of his colleague. 'Lad, I know you're bored witless, but get on with it.' He pulled himself back toward his desk and carried on with his reading, leaving his partner in a stunned silence.

'Thank you, yes, that would be great.' Melanie walked through the office with her phone pressed to her ear, ignoring her bickering juniors. 'Thanks very much, Dr Addair, we'll be here all day unless there's a development. ... Yes. Brilliant. ... Bye now.'

'Hilda Addair?' Fairer asked.

'That's the one. I've asked her to look over the conversations we've found from the dark web forums. I don't entirely get the whole forensic linguistics thing, but if we're lucky Addair might be able to spot something about the speaker that we can't.'

'Can't hurt,' Read said from behind his monitor.

'Any joy your end?' Melanie asked, looking from one to the other.

'Nothing at all, boss, I'm sorry. We're going through everything we've got, paper and screen, but every time we find a lead it goes cold soon after.' Fairer looked to his partner but Read didn't offer anything more. 'We'll keep looking, obviously, and we've got the second monitor set up in case Domdomdom logs in and starts talking again.'

Not only had the woman not checked the private message that Fairer had sent to her through the fake account, but she hadn't been online at all since they'd talked – as far as Morris had been able to tell anyway. Members of the team had been checking in every two hours at least on the off-chance that something changed, but it seemed less likely as time went on. The fact that they were yet to see her at the coffee shop had also set the investigation back on where Melanie had hoped it would be by now. Still, she tried to remain optimistic.

'You're doing everything you can. I appreciate it.'

Melanie was three paces away from her office when Morris

beckoned her. 'Boss, do you have a second?' Melanie joined her junior, pulling up an extra chair at the desk, and asked what the news was. Morris took a deep breath before starting. 'I can't find out how much she saw through the software on Ethan's laptop, but I can tell you when it was last used and it was two weeks before the murder took place.'

'Which means she hasn't been watching our investigation?'

'Exactly.'

It was a thought that had crossed Melanie's mind late last night, and she'd called Morris in a state of panic over it in the early hours of the morning to verify whether it was even a possibility. 'Thanks for checking that. It's something off the list at least.'

'I've read through the rest of Ethan's emails to the Munston account and there's nothing suspicious among them. It really was just a business transaction. The only thing I haven't been able to work out is how she paid him, assuming she did. Either way, I've sent copies of the emails over to print in case they're of use.'

Melanie wondered whether Dr Addair might be able to do something with this latest discovery. If they could find something to tie the messages from Domdomdom to the emails sent to Ethan in the first place, they might be a step closer to proving that the same woman was behind them both.

'Okay great, Morris. Is that everything?'

'For now.' She sounded disappointed.

'You're doing as much as you can. Everyone is.'

Given that she'd caught up with the majority of the team, Melanie thought she may as well check in with Carter and Burton as well. The pair had been positioned outside the coffee shop since just before it had opened that morning and, even though Melanie was sure she would have heard from them if there'd been news, she decided it couldn't hurt to check. She was a click away from hitting Carter's speed dial digit when a commotion over at Fairer's desk caught her attention.

'She's online, Morris, boss, she's...' Fairer's excitement soon quietened as he started to read the conversation script that was rolling out in front of him.

Domdomdom:
Hi straightandnarrow
I'm sorry for the silence
Real life gets in the way of things sometimes

'What do I say?' Fairer asked the room, his fingers hovering over the keyboard.

'Ask her what's been happening. That's probably the best thing to ask, right?' Read said, looking from Morris and then to Melanie, who couldn't help but narrow her eyes at him.

'Tell her that it's fine. Real life can be complicated,' Melanie suggested.

Straightandnarrow:
I get it. Real life is complicated sometimes
Domdomdom:
Very much so
Is that why you want to leave it?

'Christ, straight in,' Melanie said, reading the conversation over Fairer's shoulder. She opened her mouth to suggest a response as the dots along the bottom of the screen appeared to indicate another message was coming. 'Wait it out,' she instructed. Melanie's ringtone cut through the silence of the room and she thought she saw Read flinch at the sound. When she pulled the device out of her pocket and saw Carter's number, she sent the call to voicemail and flicked her phone on to silent;

whatever it was had to take second place to this. Unless... 'Morris, can you get Carter on the phone, or Burton?'

Morris rushed back to her desk to carry out the order.

Domdomdom:
I'm sorry if that was a touch abrupt
Straightandnarrow:
Not at all. I hadn't really thought of it as
leaving though

'What does that even mean?' Read asked over his partner's shoulder and Fairer batted away the question.

'You're doing fine, Brian,' Melanie reassured him. 'Let her lead the conversation.'

Domdomdom:
How do you see it?
Straightandnarrow:
As a good opportunity
Domdomdom:
An opportunity is a strange phrase
It's not a job offer
Straightandnarrow:
Well how would you phrase it?
Domdomdom:
One last hurrah?
Straightandnarrow:
One amazing experience?
Domdomdom:
To end all experiences
Straightandnarrow:
So what do you get out of it all?

Melanie leaned forward as though willing a reply to come. It had been a risky question but she was glad Fairer had taken the chance. The dots appeared to indicate a reply was coming and Melanie held her breath, as though the slightest disturbance might interrupt the exchange.

Domdomdom:
`What about all the things you'll miss out on?`

Fairer's shoulders dropped. 'It was worth a shot.'
'We could push her,' Read added.
'We might lose her completely if we push her,' Melanie said. It was as much a reminder to herself as it was to her colleagues. 'Slow it back down.'

Straightandnarrow:
`But how many people get to experience this?`
Domdomdom:
`Good point`
`'Well played, man, well played,' Read said,`
`his tone more reassuring.`
Domdomdom:
`So this is an experience worth dying for?`
Straightandnarrow:
`I suppose it is, yes`

Melanie watched Fairer type one message after another, and the longer she watched the more it became clear that his hands were shaking a little more with each message. She bit back on her professionalism long enough to give her junior a calming pat on the shoulder; from that gesture alone she could feel the growing tension in his shoulders. 'I'm fine, boss, really, I'm fine,' he told her, but he wasn't doing a good impression of it.

'Mel,' Morris called from her desk, and Melanie snapped around. 'You're going to want to take this. It's Carter. Our woman is at the coffee shop.'

Melanie turned back to the computer screen. 'Forget what I said. Push.'

35

'Fairer, you keep that woman talking as long as you possibly can,' Melanie shouted across the room, with Morris' desk phone still pressed to her ear. 'Carter, I want eyes on her at all times. If she shows any signs of movement then you grab her, understood?'

'Why aren't we grabbing her now?' Carter's tone was urgent, even panicked.

'Because I want something in writing.'

From across the room Melanie could hear bursts of tapping followed by lulls of quiet where the three DCs simply stared down the monitor. But Morris shouted out each response as they came in while Melanie held a half-dialogue with Carter. 'She's just sitting there like any other person in the shop,' Carter said, his tone shifting from urgent to shocked and back again with every detail he described.

'She's asking what Fairer's experience with snuff is,' Morris said.

'Feed her some of the stuff we found. Urban myth, sexual stimulant,' Melanie said, her orders disjointed. 'Still nothing?'

'Boss, maybe we haven't even got the right woman here,' Carter suggested.

'We don't have time for this, Carter.'

'I'm serious. She's bold as brass sitting there, drinking her coffee like this is all normal.'

'If she understood that this isn't normal then she wouldn't be doing it,' Burton snapped from the background. 'Bugger this.' Melanie heard the car door open and bang close again.

'What's she doing?'

'I've no idea, but she's heading for the shop.'

'So, you've never been hurt before,' Morris shouted again.

'Not in a way that could cause permanent damage,' Fairer said, reading his reply aloud as he typed it.

Down the phone Melanie heard the same open and close of a door.

'She's ordered food. We've got time,' Burton said, loud enough for Melanie to hear, and she smiled at her junior's forward-thinking. She heard the ping of another message come through and looked over to the small team.

'Permanent damage is an interesting way of saying death.'

'Tell her you're ready for it,' Melanie said, and Fairer typed. 'We're pushing her as much as we can but this is going to take time,' she said into the phone. 'If anything at all happens, any signs of movement, then you call me.' She disconnected the phone and crossed the room to stand behind Fairer as he waited for the response.

Domdomdom:
If you want to die so much then why don't you just do it yourself?

'Irwill didn't get any of this shit,' Read snapped.

'But with Ethan she took her time. We're hurrying her. We

might unnerve her doing it this way,' Morris said, looking to her superior.

Melanie gripped a hand in her hair and paced away from the desk. She took five long strides across the office to bring her level with the window in the opposite wall. Through the glass she could see the car park, marked vehicles hurrying in and out; beyond that, she could see the mess of the city. She imagined what those uniformed officers were rushing out to: domestic violence, suicide attempts, robberies, a plethora of heartache in one form or another for however many people. She exhaled hard before crossing back to the desk, her pace more hurried.

'Tell her you don't want to die. You want to be killed.'

Fairer typed the words out exactly as Melanie had said them and the reply was instant.

Domdomdom:
Then we can make a deal

Morris' desk phone started to ring in the background and without instruction the officer moved to take the call. 'It's Burton,' she announced to the room, but no one moved their stare from the screen. 'Okay, okay, that's good. ... Yep, thanks for letting us know.' She crossed back to join her colleagues, sharing the update as she walked, 'Apparently her food just touched down. Burton said she's picking at it, slow-paced. We're doing okay.'

'What do we actually need?' Read asked his superior.

'What do you mean?'

'To move on her. What do we need?'

'We need something that actually incriminates her, Read,' she replied, as though it was completely obvious. 'All we've got so far is a nod to the fact she's done this recently. Any one of us could say the same thing and it wouldn't be true.'

'You want a written confession for Ethan,' Morris said, as though filling in the blanks of Melanie's explanation.

The DI nodded. 'Exactly.'

Straightandnarrow:
Can you tell me about the last time you
did it?
Domdomdom:
What do you want to know?
Straightandnarrow:
Did he suffer?
Domdomdom:
No. But I can do that if you want
Straightandnarrow:
Have you done that before?
Domdomdom:
Sexually, or for snuff?
Straightandnarrow:
Snuff

'You're doing great, lad,' Read said, giving his partner a reassuring rub on each shoulder, as though encouraging him to take a shot in sport. 'Remember all those nights when we were rookies, and we'd try to impress women, do you remember that?'

'Is that helping?' Morris asked, her tone flat.

'Weirdly, it is a little,' Fairer said, his lips lifting at the edge to crack a smile.

'This is the longest we've waited for a reply,' Melanie said, pulling their attention back. 'Morris, get ready to call Burton, would you? If we've spooked her then they need to be ready to tail her out of there. I'm not letting her go now.'

Morris crossed to her desk as the dots appeared to show a message was incoming.

Domdomdom:

Yes, I've made people suffer for snuff. I
don't usually, but if they ask

Straightandnarrow:

So how many have suffered?

Domdomdom:

You ask a lot of questions

'Push,' Melanie said again.

Straightandnarrow:

I want to know you're for real

Domdomdom:

Okay

There has been a mixture of quiet ones and
ones who wanted to suffer

Not that I should even be telling you this

Straightandnarrow:

Why are you? What makes me so special?

Domdomdom:

Nothing. I'm just in a hurry

Straightandnarrow:

Why?

Domdomdom:

You only get so many whys before it gets
boring

Straightandnarrow:

I'm trusting you with my life here
The least you could do is tell me more about
yourself

Domdomdom:

Okay. I'm in a hurry because I'm going
away soon

```
This might be my last chance to do this for a
while
```

'Does she know we're on to her?' Read asked, looking from the screen to his superior.

Melanie narrowed her eyes at the conversation script. 'It could be a ploy, something to move Fairer along with their plans. Try to lead, Brian.' She squeezed her junior's shoulder. 'Push her for her own experiences. If she runs, we'll catch her.'

Straightandnarrow:
```
How many have there been before me?
```
Domdomdom:
```
Is this an ego thing?
...
A few. I've snuffed a few before
```
Straightandnarrow:
```
And how do I know that's true?
```
Domdomdom:
```
You'll have to trust me
```

Fairer started to type a reply but Melanie gave a tap on his shoulder to pause him. 'Give her a second, would you?' Melanie asked. 'If she wants this, she'll push, and then we'll know whether she's on to us or whether she's planning something else.'

'Like killing Fairer?' Read said, his tone too light for a conversation so dark. Melanie tried to hold back a frown; it wasn't the time for reprimands.

Domdomdom:
```
Do you watch the news?
```
Straightandnarrow:

```
Of course I do
Why?
```
Domdomdom:
```
You've seen the video then
The one of the man dying
```
Straightandnarrow:
```
Everyone has by now I should think
```
Domdomdom:
```
What do you think of it?
Does the camera get my best side?
```

'Keep her busy,' Melanie said, her tone firm. She pulled her mobile phone from her front pocket and hit the speed dial for Carter's number. He answered on the first ring. 'We've got what we needed. Bring her in, and make sure you pack up the computer with you.'

36

The woman could have been anyone. Melanie stood behind the mirrored glass and stared into the room that was now holding their prime suspect, and the woman had absolutely nothing remarkable about her. She didn't look the type for anything along these lines, and Melanie wondered whether that was the exact reason she'd got away with it until now. When Burton and Carter brought her into the station, they informed Melanie that not only had the woman not put up a struggle, she also hadn't said a single word from coffee shop to cell – nor to now, despite Melanie's brief entrance into the interview room where she offered their suspect a tea or a coffee, in the interest of striking a conversation. The killer had given Melanie a blank stare before looking back to a fixed point on the wall.

'Look what we have here,' Burton said as she stepped into the darkened room. She held three United Kingdom driver's licences fanned out like cards in front of her chest, and she left them long enough for Melanie to take in each one.

'Violet Preston.' Melanie looked from the IDs back to the woman in the interview room. 'So, that's who you are, is it?'

'These aren't the only Munston and Linwood IDs that she

had on her either, so it's hardly a fluke that she's been caught with them. Fairer and Read are running all the checks they can on the details we've got for the Preston one though, including the home address that the licence is registered to.'

'And Morris?'

Burton smiled. 'She's having a field day with the stuff on that laptop.' She matched her superior's stare and looked into the room. 'Are you going to try for a formal interview?'

'We're going to have to. If she expects to get representation then she's going to have to ask for a phone call at some point. Send Carter down here, would you? We may as well get this mess started.'

Melanie formally introduced herself for the benefit of the recording equipment that was fitted inside the room, and Carter followed. There was a heavy pause while both officers waited for the prisoner to follow their lead but nothing came.

'Could you introduce yourself for the benefit of the recording equipment, please?' Melanie asked, her tone neutral and non-threatening. The question was a polite formality; she'd decided all their interviews with the woman would be videoed, to cover themselves for anything coming their way. But despite her resolve to keep a level head, she already felt a pang of irritation at the woman's obstinance. 'We have reason to believe that you are living under the name of Violet Preston. Is that the best name to use for you, or would Munston or Linwood be more appropriate for the proceedings?'

The suspect flinched briefly at the sound of the surnames, but she didn't offer a verbal reply.

Melanie continued, 'We have reason to believe that you've been involved in a number of murders over a stretch of time.

It would be helpful if we could have a conversation about that, to at least determine whether we're talking to the right person.' Her tone was tight and although she tried to sound unmoved she was aware her words were sharp around the edges.

'Do you recognise this man at all?' Carter said, as he pulled a headshot of Ethan Irwill from a light brown folder. He set the image on the table and pushed it across until it sat in front of the woman's folded arms.

She looked down for four, five, six seconds and then looked back at Carter. She shook her head.

'Could you give a verbal response, please, for the recording equipment?'

'No, he doesn't.'

'This man, he doesn't seem familiar at all?'

'Still no.'

'He was recently murdered in the interest of making a snuff film.' Melanie let the comment hang there before she added, 'Are you at all familiar with the idea of snuff films?' The woman shifted her gaze from the table and looked Melanie straight in the eye; she blinked three times, then looked back to the point that she'd stared at previously, and Melanie had to swallow down the urge to slam her palm flat against the surface that separated them. She nudged Carter beneath the table before she said, 'Okay, I think that's enough for the time being. Interview terminated at four fifteen.'

Both of the officers stood to exit the room, but they were stunned still by the sound of the woman's voice from behind them.

'I believe I'm allowed a phone call at some point. I'd like to make that now.'

Melanie turned to face the woman but – either through childish spite, or a greater amount of self-control than she'd given herself credit for – she chose not to offer any kind of response.

Melanie dropped Carter in the main reception of the station to make arrangements for their prisoner to make a phone call. But Melanie needed a breather, and by the time she'd powered up the four flights of stairs to their office she could feel herself settling back to a normal temper. She pushed through the door into the communal space and was hit by a wall of action. Fairer and Read were swapping papers between themselves, their phones pressed to their ears; Burton was working at what looked like Ethan's laptop while Morris was half-working on what Melanie assumed must be Violet's, while also holding a hurried conversation with someone on her mobile. They weren't wasting any time, and even though Melanie felt deflated by the exchange – or lack of – with their suspect, the urgency of her team buoyed her.

'Where are we?' she said, starting with Fairer and Read.

'Very, very close to having her last registered address,' Read said, covering the phone's speaker. 'I'm just waiting on – yes, hello, I'm still here.' He held up a single index finger to his superior who moved along to check on the next officer.

Melanie came to a halt behind Morris, who had finished her phone call. She appeared to be entirely focused on the screen in front of her, with pop-up boxes appearing and disappearing at such a speed that Melanie couldn't read their contents. From the corner of her eye she saw Burton abandon Ethan's laptop, so Melanie grabbed the newly free chair and sat down next to Morris.

'What's happening here?'

She sighed. 'I've gained access to some of her dark web software, which means we can at least verify that it was definitely this woman who Fairer was talking to.'

'Which is a good thing, Morris.'

'I know, I know,' she said, her tone impatient. 'But she's got everything encoded or encrypted or en-something, and it's near impossible to do even the most basic of searches without a password box popping up.'

'But you're an expert in hacking passwords these days.' Melanie tried to sound upbeat, but she knew her team were feeling the pressure to find something. 'Do you want to call tech in?'

'I really don't. The woman is just good with this stuff but there's no reason why I can't match her.' There was a determination, a certain grit in Morris' voice that Melanie was proud of. 'Another half an hour, that's all I'll need.'

'Do whatever you can. Okay?' Melanie stood.

'How did you get on with her downstairs?'

Melanie rolled her eyes. 'We didn't. She won't answer any questions and the first that she's said to anyone was that she wanted to make a phone call.'

'Anyone suddenly miss our copycat?' Morris asked, her tone lightening.

'Yes,' Fairer shouted from across the room, and Melanie felt grateful for the beat of humour. She turned away from Morris' desk to make her way to her own but bumped straight into Burton who was holding several sheets of paper together.

'Did it work?' Morris asked, craning round her superior to her colleague.

'Did what work?' Melanie said.

'Oh, it worked.' Burton turned the paperwork to face her superior, so the top sheet was readable. While Melanie scanned the information, Burton spoke to Morris, 'The scrambler cracked it open as soon as I connected the laptops together. You were right.'

'These documents were linked across the two computers?' Melanie asked, half-understanding Burton's meaning.

Morris stood to join her colleagues. 'We weren't getting anywhere with the password scrambler on the second document that Ethan had protected. After some strategic searches, I found software keys.'

'And for the idiots at the back...' Melanie said.

'It's a security measure, a way of making sure that a document isn't tampered with from one computer to another. In pairing the computers we made a loop between both versions of the document, and both keys, which tricked the software into unlocking.'

'Morris, you're bloody brilliant.'

'Find something in there that'll help first,' she replied.

'Easy,' Burton replied. 'The final sheet is signed and dated by Ethan Irwill, of sound body and mind, and a Violet M. Linwood.'

37

Burton stared into the office where Hilda Addair was working. The doctor had arrived two hours ago and Melanie had ushered her into an empty room, wielding a pack of paperwork that she eventually left the other woman to look through. Burton watched as she made notes, magnified letters, and held various documents alongside each other – but Burton's main job was to make sure nothing left the room when the doctor did. 'She's a nice woman,' Melanie said, 'but we can't trust anyone with the fine details of a case like this.'

Addair hadn't taken out a single electronic device while she'd been in the room, so Burton could at least be sure there wouldn't be stray pictures on the loose.

'She's been in there a while,' Melanie said, coming to stand alongside her colleague.

'Whatever she's doing, she's certainly putting a fair effort in.'

'It's for selfish means. Don't be too impressed.'

Burton was shocked by her boss' tone. 'You don't like the woman?'

'She unsettles me. I worry she's in this for the glory of being an expert witness.'

'But she is an expert,' Burton said, her tone questioning.

'That's what they tell me.'

Addair looked up to catch the eyes of both women and she beckoned them into the room. The office held the heat of a space that's been sealed for too long, and Burton wondered how the woman had even managed to work in there – but she clearly had. There were notes spread out across the table along with the documents that Melanie had provided: extracts from the forum, signatures from the driver's licence, signatures from the contract with Ethan, and a handwritten note Fairer had found tucked inside an estate agent's folder, thanks to some careful snooping. Both Fairer and Read had hounded down local companies as soon as they'd found a digital footprint for Violet Preston, and the pair were sure this folder detailed her most recent address. 'Leave the note; get a team to the house,' Melanie had instructed, before filling Burton in on her plans for the handwriting.

'Is this the handwriting of a monster?' Addair asked Melanie as she stopped level with the end of the desk. Burton saw an awkward glance pass between the women, but it seemed to go unacknowledged by her superior.

'You tell me.' Melanie shifted around the table to sit opposite the doctor. 'Can you make a connection between any of this?'

Addair picked up the conversation extracts. 'I need something more to compare these to. In isolation, I can't tell you a huge amount about the person who wrote them because there just isn't enough digital material here.' She set those sheets to one side and quickly re-arranged the collection of signatures and handwriting so they sat in a row in front of her. 'However, I'd bet you good money that these are written by the same person.'

'You're sure?'

'Sure enough to bet a pricey dinner on it, if you are.'

Burton heard the playful tone sitting underneath Addair's comment and she tried to stop herself from reacting to it. But she'd never seen her boss quite so flustered.

'Okay. Ah. If we can get a larger sample, of the chatroom stuff–'

'There's every chance I'll be able to tell you a little more, DI Watton. That said, I can also tell you that you're best leading with the handwriting.'

Melanie looked taken aback. 'Because?'

'Because anyone could have written this.' She tapped the forum printouts. 'Forensic linguistics can't match digital text to handwriting. At least, not in this format. I can tell you that the same person wrote all of the messages, but that doesn't mean the same person owns these signatures.'

'I see.' Melanie stood from the table. 'Thanks for your time, Dr Addair, this has been really helpful. Are you able to send an invoice to the station when the case is closed? We can notify you when our investigation is wrapping up.'

Burton noted the curt formality her superior was trying to maintain, and from Addair's expression she'd noticed it too. The doctor gave a short giggle as she stood from her seat and grabbed her bag from the corner of the table. She extended a hand to Melanie, the furniture a safe barrier between them, and the DI reciprocated the gesture.

Mid-shake Dr Addair leaned in and said, 'I'll forget the invoice, but let's do dinner.' She pulled away before Melanie could reply and, without offering Burton the same courtesy of a handshake, she said, 'DC Burton, it's been a pleasure.'

'Likewise,' Burton replied, the beginnings of a smirk distorting the word.

Melanie turned to watch the doctor through the door of the office and eventually out of the main door of the communal space. Without turning to address Burton, she said, 'Not a word of this to anyone.'

Burton smiled. 'Yes, boss.'

Carter walked down the carpeted stairs, sending a series of soft thuds around their suspect's quiet house. They'd been here for over two hours and they had double the number of boxes to cart back to the station than when they'd found Ethan's own stash of paperwork. Fairer and Read were still sifting through cardboard containers that were scattered around the house, while the PCs that Carter had brought in as extra hands were busy with the heavy lifting.

'There's nothing upstairs, so if you want to take a break after this you're welcome to,' Carter instructed the workers as he came to a halt at the bottom of the steps. He rounded the hallway into the living room, where Fairer and Read were busy ripping open lids like children hungry for their Christmas presents. 'Is that all of the paperwork you've found, the stuff that's out there?'

Read looked around. 'There are still some boxes in here we haven't been through, but that's all we've come across that looks worth taking in.'

'Worth taking in because...?'

'One box looks to be full of deeds to houses,' Fairer said, not looking up from the papers that were in front of him.

'What, houses she owns?' Carter asked.

'It was hard to say.' Fairer discarded the sheets he'd been holding and looked up at his superior. 'Some were in her names, some weren't. We'll have to sift through and work out who owns what when we're back at the station.'

Carter eyed up the boxes that hadn't been looked through. 'Okay, where can I start?'

Read directed him over to the corner. Between the three of them they decided that if Carter went in one direction, while Fairer and Read moved in another, they'd meet in the middle somewhere along the way. The small team silently sifted through paper after paper, box after box, until the doorway was blocked up with more containers for the PCs to wedge into the evidence van. Every time Carter saw a box added, or even added a box himself, he had to swallow down a sigh at the thought of yet more paperwork to read through. But if it got the job done then it was worth it, he tried to remind himself.

Fairer and Read had stepped outside for their allotted five-minute break leaving Carter behind with a box marked *Misc.* He dragged his pocketknife along the sealed centrefold of the cardboard structure and pulled apart the lips. It was another box of papers, that much was clear. However, the first sheet was the most interesting one Carter had seen so far. In bold capital letters, ETHAN IRWILL – CONTRACT was written across the first piece of paper. Carter separated it from the sheet underneath and saw that it was the cover of the infamous kill contract; Violet's own signed copy, he assumed. He leafed through until he reached the final page and then set the bundle down alongside him. But there were more papers beneath it, with more bold names.

Carter pulled his phone from his back pocket and thumbed down to Melanie's number, half-watching his phone but half-watching the sheets as he quickly flicked through them, making a rough head count as he went.

'How are you getting on?' Melanie answered.

'Boss, I've got a whole box of contracts here.'

Melanie was silent for a beat. 'Contracts like Ethan's contract?'

'At first glance, it looks that way.'

'What's a whole bunch, Carter? How many are we talking?'

Carter glanced through the piles of paper he'd made around himself to double-check the number. 'Eleven. There are ten other contracts.'

38

Carter pushed through the single door into the Missing Persons office and scanned the herd of bodies that greeted him. By chance DS Ken Fern was the first face that he settled on, and the pair exchanged a cutting look. Carter still hadn't forgiven him for his obstruction of last year's big case. He looked away, not wanting to invite any verbal confrontation with the DS, and he resumed his scan of the room. He recognised Linden as soon as he saw her, and her flash of recognition as she saw him was a reassurance. He kept his head down and moved from one side of the room to the other, clutching a folded sheet of paper tight in his palm.

'DS Carter, this is a nice surprise,' Linden said, but then frowned. 'I mean, it's a nice surprise to see you. Given that you're probably here for bad reasons, it's not...' she trailed off, and Carter found the clumsy greeting quite endearing.

'I need your help,' he said. 'Again.'

Linden gestured towards her desk and let Carter lead the way. The pair pulled up two chairs, pressed close together in a vain attempt at creating some privacy in the open-plan office.

'It's okay. There's been a big break on some case or another and everyone is too busy to care about much else today,' Linden said, as though noting Carter's hesitation.

'We've got quite a big case going on upstairs too.'

'Sure, the snuff video, right?'

Her abruptness shocked him. 'Right.' He pulled the list from his pocket and unfolded it, but kept the names facing his chest. 'We've got reason to believe that there might be other men, other victims involved in the case. I have names.'

'And you need a search or two?' Linden filled in the blank. She held out her hand to take the paper from him and Carter handed it over. He saw her eyes widen a fraction at the length of the list. 'Or ten.'

'You don't have to search for them all if it's too–'

'It's not too anything. This is literally my job.' She smiled, and then set about inputting names and searching through details. It only took ten minutes to verify that three of the names on the sheet were individuals who had been registered as missing – dating back as far as four years.

'This guy.' Linden gestured to a name on the screen. 'Neil Quinton had people checking on his case for a while.'

'Checking how?'

Linden skimmed the screen. 'The person who reported him missing, a Wesley Orton, a work colleague by the looks of things, was calling every week at one point for an update on the case, then every month, then it drops again...'

Carter's stomach turned at the thought of the other seven reports showing up similar results.

Melanie and Burton entered the interview room with all eleven contracts safe inside folders, ready for the big reveal. Their next job would be to go through the documents with a fine-tooth comb. *But for now*, Melanie thought, *the least these papers are good for was rattling their silent suspect.* The woman had been given more than enough time with her legal representation; a Xander Hodder, who Melanie knew through reputation alone. He was younger than she expected, but when she seated herself in front of him he flashed her the smug expression of a man who's been around the courtroom a few times. He didn't look in the least bit concerned to be in an interview room – and neither did his client. Melanie and Burton introduced themselves for the purposes of the recording equipment and left a beat of silence for their interviewee to do the same.

'Violet Preston.' Her tone was flat, unfazed.

'Xander Hodder.'

'Miss Preston, you're aware that you've been brought here today to discuss your involvement in the death of Ethan Irwill,' Melanie started, but Hodder soon held up a hand to prevent her from continuing.

'There's a presupposition there that my client is guilty.'

'Surely, Mr Hodder, if we thought she was innocent then there wouldn't be much point in us having brought her here to begin with.' Melanie flashed a tight smile; a dare for him to continue, but to her pleasant surprise he backed down. 'Does the name Ethan Irwill mean anything to you?'

Violent glanced to Hodder and looked back to Melanie. 'No comment.'

Melanie stifled a quiet sigh. 'Are you at all aware of the recent footage that's been discovered, which shows Ethan's death taking place on film?'

'No comment.'

'Do you have any existing knowledge of snuff films, or the culture around them?'

'No comment.'

Melanie threw Hodder a sharp look.

'Ah, you'll have spotted that I've advised my client not to answer your questions for the time being, given that we're unsure of the evidence you'll be using against her.'

'It's our privilege not to divulge details of the evidence this early in an interview.'

'And it's Miss Preston's privilege to decline to answer your questions.'

'Okay,' Melanie started again, her tone harder. 'We have reason to believe that you murdered Ethan Irwill as part of a kill-on-demand contract, which was negotiated for the purpose of making a snuff film. We have evidence to support this already, so it would make our lives, and yours,' she paused to throw a pointed glance at Hodder, 'much easier if you would co-operate with our investigations.'

'What evidence do you have?' Hodder jumped in.

'DNA samples were taken from your client when she was initially processed here at the station. The results from that will place her at the crime scene, we're sure, and at the victim's house. A handwriting analysis has already been completed that shows the signature on Ethan's contract and the signatures on your client's multiple driver's licences – we'll come to those charges a little later – were all signed by the same individual too, namely, your client.'

Hodder tapped Violet on the arm. 'They have nothing. Say nothing.'

'Mr Hodder–'

'DI Watton, you're basing all of this on a handwriting sample and a DNA match that you haven't made yet. You'll have to forgive me if I don't advise my client to put her wrists out.'

'We also have reason to believe that Ethan Irwill is not your client's first victim,' Burton said.

'Supported by explicitly worded contracts, with your client's name on them,' Melanie added.

Violet's eyes stretched wide. It was the first clear reaction Melanie had spotted.

'Contracts?' Hodder repeated, his emphasis falling on the plural.

Melanie and Burton took alternate turns heaving files from the floor and onto the table, until there were eleven separate brown folders overlapped between themselves and their opposition. Burton opened the cover of the one closest to her – with a strategic 'one' scribbled in the corner, for this very moment – and pulled out the first sheet in the contractual agreement made between Violet and Ethan. She turned the sheet to face the suspect.

'This is one of eleven contracts that we found when we searched your home earlier today. In this, and in the others, you appear to have negotiated terms to murder the other participant in each contract. Do you have anything to say in response to that?' Burton's tone was firm, confident.

Hodder set his hand on Violet's arm. 'Eleven?'

Melanie wasn't sure whether the question was directed at her, Burton, or even Violet, so the DI answered herself. 'Yes, Mr Hodder, eleven separate contracts where your client appears to have negotiated the terms for killing another human. Do either of you have anything to say?'

'They were of sound mind when they signed those contracts,' Violet snapped, her voice cracked from under-use in the hours before this.

'Violet, not a word,' Hodder cautioned.

'It looks a lot like these men who were of sound mind, and who also wanted to die, were also happy to sign over their houses to you a month or two ahead of them dying. Except Ethan Irwill, that is, who actually made a will. Was there a reason you did things differently this time?' Melanie pushed and, rather than watching Violet, she watched Hodder. The man's eyes narrowed as he looked across the contract, his lips moving quickly although no sound emerged from them. He looked as though he was trying to battle arithmetic and failing. 'We've got some missing pieces along the way, unfortunately, which you might be able to help with. For example, these men were presumably registered as missing at one time or another.'

'But no one seems to have batted an eyelid at you having gained access to their financials.' Burton almost sounded playful as she finished off Melanie's comment. 'How did you manage that?'

'We're not going to do the investigation for you,' Hodder said.

'For murder we can hold a suspect for much longer, especially with the evidence we've got.' Melanie took the folder from Burton and stacked it on top of another, repeating this process until there were two separate piles for her and her colleague to carry. 'We'll build the case, Mr Hodder, and I suspect that once we get started your client will actually make it quite easy for us.' She shifted her gaze to look directly at Violet then. 'I imagine that after ten you must get quite cocksure; especially cocksure, to let a victim make an official will.'

Melanie and Burton formally excused themselves from the interview and stood from the table, grabbing a pile of contracts each. It wasn't until Melanie was facing the door that Hodder pulled her back into the room with another question.

'You won't mind me asking, for clarity, that is, whether those ten men are all missing persons?'

'We're in the process of verifying their missing persons' status, but we have reason to believe already that at least a sample of them are, yes.'

He tapped his knuckles twice on the desk and smiled. 'Good

news for our case then.'

'And why's that?' Burton asked.

'Good luck proving eleven murders with only one body.'

39

Melanie kicked open the door to the communal space, with Burton trailing in behind her. The door clattered back into the adjacent wall, pulling in the attention of those working in the office. Melanie saw Burton gesture to them, a signal to keep quiet, and she was grateful for a beat of time to herself before she had to explain the outburst. She paced over to the evidence board and stared down the mismatches of information that had been added to and edited near-constantly in the last few weeks. There had to be something they were missing.

She turned to address the team. 'Violet Preston has an exceptionally good lawyer who is going to argue that we can't prove eleven murders with only one body, and he's right.'

'But we've got bloody contracts,' Carter said.

'Circumstantial.'

'Is it though?' Burton questioned. 'I mean, surely there's a clear intent there?'

'They're not worth the paper they're written on without a body, and that's why he knows that Ethan's is the only murder we can take Violet down for.' Melanie dropped onto a seat near an abandoned desk; she leaned on the surface next to her, with her forehead resting heavy in her hand. Something had to give. 'We need to find something that can prove she murdered the other men, if we plan on sending her down for it all.'

Carter stepped into the centre of the room. 'Okay, here's a start. DC Linden down in the missing persons department did a check on the names we have. Seven out of the ten are registered as missing; four of those were reported missing by people at work, rather than people in their personal lives.'

'She targets loners,' Burton said.

'Exactly. The three who haven't been reported missing also haven't used their bank accounts, their national insurance numbers, or anything else that could identify them for upwards of two years now. People even stopped looking for them.'

'But someone did look for them?' she asked.

Carter looked down at his notes. 'Someone looked for one of them, a Neil Quinton who was reported missing by a work colleague.' He skimmed further down the page. 'There are so many goddamn names here. Got it: Wesley Orton. He called every week or so, then dropped it to every month, to see whether there was news.'

'Is he still calling?'

'There's nothing in the case file to suggest that he is.'

'So, the one person who had someone doesn't really have someone?' Burton sighed.

'Don't look so glum, Burton, there's a final piece...' he trailed off and span around to point to Fairer and Read who were hunched over a shared computer screen.

Fairer straightened up to address the room on cue. 'The three men who aren't registered as missing all transferred their houses over to Violet Linwood or Munston in the months before their credentials were last used anywhere. Read and I managed to find the paper trail for the property transfers.'

'Lads, I could kiss you.' Melanie stood and walked back to

the evidence board. In shorthand she added in the information that her team had found, before she turned back. 'And what about the seven that are officially missing?'

'No one is looking for them, boss,' Carter said, and Melanie thought he sounded genuinely sad. 'Even the three who were reported missing by friends, rather than colleagues, no one has checked on those cases since a month or two after they were registered.'

'Okay, and the rest of their houses?'

'We're working on that,' Fairer said. 'But we've got a few addresses to get started.'

'How far do these cases and contracts go back?' Burton asked.

Morris took her turn in addressing room. 'Seven years ago is the earliest one.'

'Fucking Christ.'

Melanie scanned the room and guessed that the eruption had come from Read. His eyes were narrowed, as though inspecting something, and Melanie had to admit the more they learned about this case the harder she found it to understand as well.

'Okay, we've got two main lines of enquiry going forward, so tune in.' She tried to steady her tone. The team needed jobs, a clear direction to get through the coming hours. 'First, we need to know what makes Ethan different. The big issue with Violet and Ethan's plan is that she was named, sort of, in his will as the executor; that was her first mistake, we think. The second mistake was letting that film be seen by eyes other than her own. I don't care whether you have to strip that machine down to nothing,' she said, directing the comment at Morris, 'or whether you read those contracts until you can recite them, we need to know what made Ethan different. Why was she prepared to get caught for him?' Melanie turned as though she'd finished but then span back. 'Are there copies of these contracts on her laptop somewhere?'

'I've found a couple of them. She's got them scattered, I'd guess in case someone hacked a single folder or file. She's a smart woman,' Morris said, sounding more irritated than impressed.

'We need to know if the printed documents and the digital ones actually match.'

'You think they won't?' Carter asked.

'I've no idea, but we've missed things with this woman already and I'm not leaving a stone unturned now. Films,' she said, clicking her fingers. 'Are there more films?' There was another expletive eruption from somewhere in the room, but Melanie let it pass. 'If she kept a copy of Ethan's film there's every possibility she kept others, so we need to be looking for them.'

The team nodded along with Melanie's comments but there was a pregnant pause sitting heavy in the room when she'd finished.

'Are they the second lines of enquiry?' Burton asked.

Melanie looked at the pile of contracts stacked in the centre of the room. 'If only. We need to find the other ten bodies.'

It was three hours later when Fairer tapped his knuckles against Melanie's open door. The whole office had been quiet for so long that the noise felt like a real disruption. Melanie looked up, along with Carter and Burton who had been working alongside her in trying to decipher the fine details of housing deeds, fake certificates and everything else they'd unearthed so far. Despite being at it for hours, Melanie didn't feel as though they were any closer to seeing any fine details or spotting trickery, and she was glad of a momentary distraction. She gestured Fairer into the room and he took two strides in, holding a stack of papers in front of him.

'I've got a theory.'

'We'll take any theories you've got,' Melanie replied. 'Carter, grab another chair.'

With the four officers sitting around the desk, Fairer launched into his explanation. 'Read and I have been talking over the afternoon about the bodies, the victims. Read's train of thought was if you were going to hide a body, where would you leave it?' He paused here as though waiting for Melanie to answer.

'I'm not hearing a theory,' she said.

'Realistically, I'd want to hide it somewhere I could keep an eye on it,' Burton said. She flashed Fairer a sympathetic look.

'Or somewhere miles away from where you'll ever have to deal with it,' Carter added. 'They'd be the two extremes, wouldn't they? You either want it on your doorstep or you want it as far away from you as possible.'

'Exactly.' Fairer flopped the pile of papers onto the desk and Melanie saw they were printouts for the victims' houses.

She spotted the theory. 'Fairer, you're a bloody genius.'

'As far as we can tell Violet got a hold of each house before the victims went missing, and she kept a hold of each house until the victims were reported missing, meaning, she sat on the properties until such a time that the police might have got involved. Not that we did, but... Anyway, after that point paperwork dries up entirely and before you know it the house is registered to someone else. The only exception being the victims who weren't registered as missing, where she seems to have kept a hold of the properties for longer.'

'What do you mean the paperwork dries up?' Burton asked.

'Morris is looking into it, but we can only track the paperwork up to a certain point and then it goes cold, which is probably why she's never been pulled up.'

Melanie ran a hand down over her face. 'She's been hacking into the right places and tampering with documents, that's what we're thinking?'

'It's for Morris to say but it looks to us like that's the case. Read is out there explaining the same theory to her now to see what digging she can do.'

Carter shifted the papers along the desk to get a good view of them all alongside each other. 'So, this is what we're thinking now? The bodies, they're in the houses still?'

'Or under them,' Fairer said, with the smugness of someone delivering a good punchline. 'We looked into planning permissions and building records for the times the men went missing. We're still waiting to hear back from some of them but at this stage it's a good theory, we think.' Fairer seemed to lose someone of his confidence as he locked eyes with Melanie across the desk. But the DI nodded her head; this was their new leading theory.

'Burton, call forensics and tell them we're going to need their help with several searches and body retrievals in the coming days, tell them anyone they can spare would be appreciated. Carter, get downstairs and see if you can round up some uniformed bodies to come and help with the grunt work. There might be some hard labour ahead for the rest of today, and for a few days, I'd say.' She looked at Fairer. 'You up for some digging?'

He flashed a quick smile. 'Where do we start?'

Melanie looked down at the snapshots of properties spread out over the desk.

'Good question...'

40

Morris was well into reading the seventh contract and she knew by heart what the terms and conditions were for each arrangement. Every man that Violet had targeted had wanted to die, and they had wanted to have their death filmed. Morris didn't understand it, not even a little, but she could see the trouble that Violet had gone to to make sure these contracts were as clear as they could possibly be, and Morris was both irritated and impressed by the killer's level of care. She looked down at her checklist of terms before she skipped ahead to Ethan's contract. She was yet to read it in full – she'd wanted to spend her time learning the ins and outs of the others first – but she felt ready now. Morris uncapped a bright yellow highlighter and set to reading and annotating the document. She was five pages into it when she spotted the first difference.

'Boss, do you have time for this?' Morris caught Melanie midway between her office and the exit, and she looked hurried. But Morris reasoned this was important enough to interrupt her superior.

Melanie looked at the door then back to Morris' desk. 'Okay, you've got five minutes. They've found something at the first site and I need to get there.'

'I'll be quick.' Morris clicked her way into two of the digital contracts saved on Violet Preston's hard drive: contract one and Ethan's contract. She pushed the keyboard back to spread out the corresponding printed pages from each contract too. 'I've been trying to work out what the difference was between Ethan and the rest of them, and then I found this.' She pointed at the page numbers, first on the screen and then on the matching contracts. Melanie spotted it instantly; the final print version had an additional clause.

'The property' will not be delivered to V. until the initial terms of the agreement have been met. E.'s property will therefore not be released until death has been confirmed and at such time 'the property' will be made available to V. through the terms laid out in E.'s Last Will and Testament, where it will also be noted that E. does not wish for his death to be investigated, or for V. to be pursued in any official or legal manner.

Before Melanie could answer, Morris held up a finger to direct her to another clause in the contract. 'I also found this.'

On completion of the agreement, V. will ensure that the footage is distributed across various social media and internet-based channels, and V. will also ensure that the film receives adequate media attention. On the condition that this media attention does not result in V.'s capture, or inadvertent confession, V. will gather as much attention as she possibly can to ensure E. is named as the individual in the film sequence and that details of their arrangement are made public.

'She edited the contract between print and digital versions?'

'It looks that way. They're the only differences I've spotted across all the contracts so far. I'll keep looking, but as differences go...' she petered out.

'These are key ones,' Melanie said, finishing her colleague's comment. 'So, this is why everything was different for him; he had it written into his contract? He must have known that these terms could put her in danger of being caught.'

'Of course, he must have known,' Morris agreed. 'But surely so did she?'

Carter checked his phone one last time but there was nothing from Melanie, and she hadn't answered his last three calls to the office. He walked back around the side of the house and joined Burton in the butchered back garden. The search team had only been there for an hour, but it looked as though there hadn't been a green landscape in the yard for years.

'They don't waste any time, do they?' Carter said.

Burton turned to face him. 'They don't, and we shouldn't either.'

'You think?' he asked, and she replied with a firm nod. 'Okay, chaps, keep going at the pace you're going until you can lift that thing from the ground and into a cordoned area. We'll get the medical examiner on standby.' He lowered his voice to address Burton. 'Can you call George Waller? Let him know we might have a body for him in the next half an hour.' Burton pulled her phone from her inside pocket and took a step along the marked path leading out of the garden, but Carter reached out a hand to stop her. 'On second thoughts, could you let him know there might be a few?'

Carter took a step closer to the dip in the centre of the

garden; a space that had been slowly spreading outwards while the team performed their preliminary search. They'd found something, according to the scanner that Carter didn't quite understand; something that was apparently another foot or so underneath the surface. He watched as they hacked and cut away at the land, with a swell in the centre of his stomach as he hoped for and against them finding a body. It would make their case, obviously, but it would also be the start of a ten-body hunt that Carter didn't know whether he had the stamina for. It was meant to be his weekend with Emily, starting tomorrow with a surprise school collection and a McDonald's. But the longer these investigations went on, the more Carter dreaded making that phone call to Trish to cancel his visit, something that he knew he'd never live down.

'Anything yet?' Burton said, coming to a stop alongside him, and Carter was glad of the interruption to such unpleasant thoughts.

'Not yet, but they've said it won't be long.'

'Have you heard from Mel?'

Carter pulled his phone out on the off-chance he'd missed a call. 'Still nothing.'

'They must have found something back at the station.'

'Either that or they've beaten us to it at one of the other sites,' Carter suggested.

'Fairer or Read would have called. Besides, Waller didn't mention having heard from anyone else. He's working in his office all day. He said he could be here whenever we need him, if we need him.'

'DS Carter?' A voice strained over the sound of spades hitting dirt. 'We've got something to pull up over here.'

Carter flashed Burton a raised eyebrow. 'Better let the good doctor know he's needed.'

41

Melanie stood outside Waller's office and inhaled deeply, sucking in the too-familiar scent of cleaning chemicals and death. She inhaled hard one last time and pushed open the door on the out breath. The room was a mess of discarded body bags and muddied tarpaulin, the latter of which she assumed had come straight from the different crime scenes. On four steel trolleys descending back through the room, Melanie could see four muddied male corpses in various stages of decomposition, and she had to tense her stomach to stop a heave from rising up through her. She couldn't spot Waller, so she took three strides further into the room to bring herself closer to body one. The man didn't look dissimilar to Ethan Irwill; he might have been attractive, before the earth had started to eat away at him. But he was well-built, his width and shoulders filling out the table, and his length stretching all the way to the bottom. *Violet Preston never stood a chance at physically overpowering men like this*, Melanie thought. But if the footage of Ethan's murder was anything to go by, then she'd never needed to.

The door wailed as someone pushed into the room and

Melanie span around to spot George, still wearing his overalls, his face smeared with mud in several places.

'Well, DI Watton, you certainly know how to show a man a good time.' He gave a little laugh. 'Some give roses, some give chocolates. You give...' he trailed off as he stepped around her and moved to the body at the back of the room, the fourth in line. Melanie followed him, a smile teasing the corners of her lips, although she felt dreadful for the expression.

'I can give you chocolates when this is all over,' she offered.

'Oh, you certainly will.' George snapped a glove on. 'This chap is the worst out of the bunch but fortunately for us, his cause of death is quite obvious.'

George pulled up a large spotlight and angled it over the man's head before flicking it on. Melanie flinched away from the cadaver; she couldn't help the reaction. In the far end of the office space, away from the high windows that let the light in, it had been impossible to get too clear a look at the body. But with the bare bulb staring the man straight in the face, she could see the open slash across his neck. An inch wide, it was clogged with dirt and Melanie feared what might come tumbling out when George started to investigate.

'Don't be so bashful, Mel, it doesn't suit you.'

'Sometimes, George,' she said, but didn't add anything more. She knew better than to insult someone who was about to do her a favour – or rather, a string of favours. 'Are all of the others quite as violent as this one?'

'It's too soon to tell, honestly. Number two looks to be fairly beaten up but I'll need a closer look at things to know whether that's pre or post mortem. They've been in the ground for long enough for the earth to have done damage, so it'll take some careful searching, I should think. Meanwhile, numbers one and three are more like young Ethan.'

'Stifled?'

'Stifled, suffocated, drugged. Again, I'll have to poke around further but there aren't the same outward signs that the other two have.'

Melanie sighed. 'She said she was only rough with people when they asked her to be.'

'Yes, she's quite a piece of work from what I've heard.'

'People are talking then?' Melanie couldn't keep the disappointment from her voice.

George let out a curt laugh as he pulled his surgical mask up. 'Mel, you've collared an eleven-victim-strong serial killer. Did you think people wouldn't talk?'

She tutted. 'She isn't a serial killer.'

The medical examiner held his arm outstretched to gesture at the string of bodies occupying his slabs. 'I'd beg to differ. Don't be modest. Your killer certainly won't be.'

'I have no idea what she'll be, George. She didn't want to say a word when we interviewed her the first two times.'

Waller let out a sharp huff of air. 'Yes, well, let's see what she says this time, eh?'

When Melanie walked back into her own shared office space, the lights in the room had been dimmed and the blinds to the windows pulled down. It took a careful look around the room to spot Read, Fairer, Burton and Morris crowded around a computer monitor, and the team were so fascinated with their viewing that it looked as though they hadn't heard their superior enter the room. Melanie took deliberately quiet steps from one side of the space to the other until she came to a halt one stride away from them. She was close enough to see the monitor from this viewpoint, and she suddenly understood what had the team so distracted.

There was a young man in the centre of the film frame. Melanie guessed he was early thirties at a push. He was attractive enough, with short cropped hair and an obviously muscular physique. But as his head lolled from one shoulder to another, as though looking for support to keep upright, Melanie guessed he'd had a similar treatment to Ethan Irwill – which meant there was nothing attractive about what was coming.

'You've found the videos?' Melanie asked, and there was a shared jump of surprise that moved across the four members of her team. 'I didn't mean to unsettle anyone.'

Fairer reached forward to pause the film. 'I don't think it's you that's unsettling us.'

Melanie caught Morris' eye. 'You found the footage on her laptop?'

'I eventually found them stored on an online server, which was both clever and not. These things can always be cracked into with enough determination. She must have known she was taking a chance in storing this stuff on something like that.'

Read snorted. 'Something tells me she's one for taking risks, our Violet.'

'We found something worthwhile going through her papers too,' Fairer said, tapping his partner as though to remind him. 'Read thought we might find more information about the houses but instead found a bloody binder of this stuff.' He gestured to the screen. 'Names of films, methods, rankings.'

'Rankings?' Melanie repeated, her voice raised.

'It looks like she's been studying snuff films,' Read explained. 'They're not real, we found out, but she's been watching staged ones for years by the looks of those notes. She's written down what she likes, what she doesn't like, what she might–'

'She gets it, mate, the woman wrote a lot of stuff down,' Fairer interrupted.

'Anything that'll help us build our case?'

'It'll help us build a character profile if nothing else,' Burton said. 'If you read these notes, boss, they're full of observations, suggestions, analyses. It's genuinely like she was a student of these things, before she tried to make her own.'

Melanie pulled up a chair and positioned herself behind the officers. 'And how many of these are there?'

'Morris managed to find eleven altogether, including a copy of Ethan's. She had everything stored online this whole time.'

Melanie ran a hand over her face. 'Christ, okay. Let's get started then.' Morris reached forward to re-start the film but Melanie butted in with another question, 'Why isn't Carter in on this development?'

'He had to leave to attend to some personal business,' Burton said, her tone clipped, as though she'd been rehearsing the line all afternoon.

Melanie looked down at her watch. They were, technically, all off the clock. The digs had been called to an end for the evening, with forensics and search teams set to start afresh at first light the following day. But she felt a little surprised at Carter, of all people, walking out on the biggest break of their careers. As though sensing this surprise, Burton added, 'I think it's something to do with Emily.'

Melanie gave her junior a quick smile. 'Understood. Let's get going.'

Morris hit the play button and the silent film kicked in again. In the same pattern as before, their once-mystery woman appeared on-screen to check the sturdiness of her victim. Violet was cropped out of frame, but she was visible from just beneath her breasts. The man's head tilted back against her torso while her fingers pressed at both sides of his neck, as though feeling for a weakness in the muscles. She pushed and pulled and, apparently satisfied, she placed a hand over the man's nose and over his mouth, just as she had done with Ethan. But rather than buck against her, the victim kicked into life. He grabbed at Violet's arms and pulled his nails down her skin with such a force that the woman jerked backwards, letting the man's head fall loose.

'Learning curve,' Read said. 'I wonder if this is when she started to use binds on them.'

She stepped back further away from the camera before rushing forwards and grabbing something from just in front of where her victim was seated.

'Morris, go back, would you?' Melanie asked. 'A few seconds at a time, can you do that?' Morris followed orders and clicked back frame by frame, the reverse footage playing out until, 'There, stop right there.' Morris hit the pause button and there, in the top left corner of the freeze-frame, clutching one injured arm to her chest, was a clear headshot of Violet Preston. 'Caught live on film,' Melanie said with some satisfaction. 'Two down, nine to go.'

42

The file landed with a thud on Archer's desk. Melanie dropped into the chair opposite her superior and gestured to the paperwork between them. Archer raised an eyebrow and retrieved the documents. In the last sixteen hours, Melanie's team – and the teams she'd managed to drag in to help – had found six bodies, performed three post-mortems, watched nine snuff films, and drafted seven different interview strategies. Archer was holding the relevant paperwork for everything the teams had managed to put together under pressure, and Melanie felt damn proud of what they'd achieved in the time they'd had – but she wanted more. She needed to be certain that when she walked into that room she was wearing enough body armour for battle, and she knew Archer would be her sounding board for it.

'Okay, talk me through what you're hitting her with.'

Melanie cricked her neck from one side to the other, as though loosening up for a physical confrontation. 'We've got contracts between her and every missing man, signed with her signature which an expert has already in-part verified for us. We've got films of all the murders taking place, that Morris retrieved from the suspect's laptop and online servers she'd been using. Read is in the process of tracking down the missing paperwork that will tie her to the houses by name, but the documentation that we found at her house gave us enough to take us straight to the properties anyway–'

'I've read all of this, Mel. I want to know what your ace is.'

There was one final folder tucked down the side of Melanie in her seat. She leaned to one side to free it and pulled out the image that was pressed safe inside. 'This.' She handed the photograph to her superior. The image was an improved version of the still that Morris had isolated from one of the snuff films. It showed Violet Preston, beyond reasonable doubt, and the context of the film itself was enough to prove she'd murdered the man involved.

'Caught in action?'

'Exactly. Morris is going through the other films with a fine-toothed comb to see if we can find anything similar to this again.'

'You can still only prove two murders though,' Archer said, and Melanie thought there was a tinge of judgement in her boss' voice.

'We're doing everything we can for this, ma'am.'

Archer softened her expression. 'I don't doubt it, Mel. It wasn't a criticism, just an observation. Do you think proving two is enough?'

'Honestly, I'll take two at the moment.' She dropped back against the chair behind her. 'We have enough circumstantial evidence to tie her to the other nine cases. I would hope, I have to hope, that if we can prove two beyond reasonable doubt then we can at least introduce the evidence for the others and a jury can decide whether she's guilty for them or not.'

Archer leaned forward to take another glance across the paperwork. 'Okay,' she said, looking along the sheets before shifting them slightly to inspect the documents that were over-lapping each other. 'Okay, I buy it. I think if you take it to the interview room and her brief tries to negotiate you should consider it a win.'

'You think I should make a deal?'

'No, I absolutely don't. My point is you'll know how good the case is depending on whether her representation *wants* to negotiate. Don't take anything you're offered, do you understand? We're taking this as far as we can.' Archer started to collect the papers together. 'She's a sick, sick woman, that much is clear, but there's no way we're letting her walk out of a courtroom scot-free.'

Melanie couldn't hide her relief. The majority of her team had pulled an all-nighter and the support teams had been up since first light to inspect the various crime scenes and search for more cadavers to bring home. She was grateful that she could finally take some optimism back to the officers working under her.

'Is there anything you need from me?' Archer said but before Melanie could answer Archer's desk phone started to ring. She rolled her eyes and answered, 'Hello? Ah, DC Morris. ... Yes, she's here with me still. ... Of course, I don't mind taking a message.' Her tone was playful, but Melanie couldn't under-stand how; unless the superintendent was more confident about the case than she'd let on. 'I see. ... Of course, I'll let her know. She'll be coming back up to you all shortly. ... Absolutely. ... Keep it up.' Archer set the phone down and rubbed at her eyes with her thumb and forefinger before addressing Melanie, 'Morris has finished watching the tenth snuff film that she found on the woman's computer. The worst of the bunch, apparently, but she's managed to pull a five-second clip of Violet Preston from the footage.'

Melanie smiled, understanding the implication of the news. 'And then there were three.'

The office was busy with Melanie's usual suspects, including Carter who had by the grace of God managed to find childcare for the day, and they'd been joined by faces Melanie could hardly recognise. There had been an influx of experts and experienced workers who had retrieved bodies, sampled forensics and generally liaised with the home team since everything had fully come to life, and it seemed they'd taken to walking through the office at random too. Not that Melanie minded, as long as they were getting the job done. Her first port of call now needed to be Morris, so Melanie could see for herself what kind of footage they were dealing with from this final film. But midway to Morris' desk, Melanie was intercepted by Burton.

'Graham Williams, that forensics guy, is waiting in your office.' She was juggling files as she spoke, trying to get one tray of documents to lie neatly on another, while she kept moving toward her desk.

'Good news?' Melanie asked.

In a graceless manoeuvre, Burton dropped everything onto her desk in a great heap before falling into her chair. She puffed. 'I'm sorry, boss, he didn't say. He just said it was urgent and he'd wait for you to get back.' She set about sorting through the papers without looking for a response from Melanie, so the senior officer headed to her own room.

Williams was sitting in the visitor's chair with his back facing the entrance. He must have heard her arrival because no sooner had Melanie walked through the door, he turned with a content expression to greet her.

'You look happy at least,' Melanie said, crossing the room to get to her own chair. She sat down opposite her colleague. Melanie imagined that she looked about as tired as she felt and she couldn't help but think that whatever Williams had been doing for the last twelve hours, it certainly wasn't digging up crime scenes. He looked well-rested and braced for a day. Melanie couldn't tell whether she begrudged him or judged him for his appearance.

'Nothing like being busy to set you in a good mood.'

Melanie raised at an eyebrow. 'You think?'

'Okay, maybe there are different types of busy.' He gave a half-laugh and leaned forward in his seat, closing the gap between himself and Melanie. 'I started to liaise with George Waller late in the day yesterday. He told me what the situation was here, and we thought it would be easier to run whatever we could without you and ask permission later. Given the state of the office out there...' he trailed away, and Melanie gestured her understanding.

'You did the right thing. What brings you here on this hot mess of a morning?'

Williams set a file down, flicked it open and pulled out four sheets of paper from inside. He spread them across Melanie's desk as though fanning cards. 'Cast your mind back to when this was a one-man case and we found female hair in Ethan Irwill's house and his crime scene.'

'Ah, those were the days.'

'I know we didn't match it at the time but given that it's an ongoing investigation, we kept the details to hand. Now, I've heard on the grapevine that your DC Morris has found footage that shows one of the victims scratching at your killer. Have you managed to ID the victim yet?'

Melanie shook her head. 'We should have an ID within the next day or so but it's a forest of paperwork out there.'

Williams glanced over the sheets in his bundle before

selecting one and spinning it around to face Melanie. 'Number three on Waller's slab.' Melanie's eyes widened as she connected Williams' announcement with the sheet in front of her. She didn't know much about forensics, but she knew a break in a case when she heard one. 'Waller took samples from under the victim's fingernails as part of his examination, although he forewarned us the best we'd probably find was muck.' He leaned forward to point at the various data entries on the sheet as he spoke. 'It turns out what Waller thought was dirt was actually dried blood. We were able to pull a sample and compare it to the hair that we found in the Irwill scenes.'

'It's a match?'

'It's a match.' Williams nodded. 'There are enough positive markers for a definitive ID between her, the two crime scenes and the body. Waller sent over more samples in the early hours of this morning that we haven't been able to look through yet, but as soon as we get to them I'll bring the results over myself.'

'It might be a wasted journey for you, Graham, it's best to courier as much as you can or call a uniform over.' Melanie pushed the sheet of forensics results back towards him. 'If I have it my way, I'll be tied up with an interview for most of the afternoon.'

43

Violet Preston looked notably more tired than the last time Melanie had laid eyes on her. But Hodder was the same slick lawyer; he sat straight-backed alongside the suspect, and looked as cocksure as he had done on their first meeting. Before arranging for the interview, Melanie and Carter had spent an hour going back and forth on how to approach it. After much deliberation they decided not to script their interactions. 'There's no way of knowing how she'll respond to this kind of evidence,' Melanie decided, and on seeing the state the woman appeared to be in after thirty-odd hours in a station cell, the officer thought she'd made the right call. Preston looked as though she hadn't slept, and Melanie hoped that might make her all the more vulnerable to the upcoming questions.

After the formal introductions were made again, Melanie gave Carter the nod to ask the first of their queries. 'Where did you and Ethan Irwill first meet?'

Violet looked from Carter to Hodder and back again. She opened her mouth as though to respond but seemed to think better of it when Hodder set a hand on her arm to stop her. *His token move*, Melanie thought.

'Shouldn't you be able to tell us that?'

'We're hoping your client might be able to help us with our case.'

'Please. She won't help you to build a case against her, DS Carter.'

'We already have a case against her, Mr Hodder, but there are certain gaps that we'd like filled before we decide exactly what it is your client will be charged with.'

'What are the options?' Preston asked, and Melanie thought the woman's eruption caught both men off guard, their heads snapping round at the noise. 'For what charges will be brought against me, I mean. What are the options?'

'It's too soon to say for certain,' Melanie said.

'Because you don't have enough evidence, DI Watton?' Preston asked. She sounded as though she'd picked up a touch of Hodder's tone – and Melanie wanted to knock it out of her.

'Mr Hodder, is your client likely to help us with our investigations or should we assume that she won't co-operate? Frankly, I don't have a problem with either option, but it would be good to know so we can factor in time wasted when we account for our time spent on the case.' Melanie part-regretted the outburst, but the stretch of Hodder's eyes made any consequences seem worth it already. The lawyer didn't respond so Melanie encouraged Carter to continue with his questions.

'Where did you and Ethan Irwill meet?'

Preston opened her mouth but, as though catching Hodder in her peripherals, she shook away whatever answer it was she'd been about to say. 'I don't know that Ethan Irwill and I ever did meet, detective.'

'So, if I said we'd got footage of you two together on camera, you'd say what?'

'I'd say you must be mistaken.'

Melanie watched Hodder nod slowly, as though giving

Preston's answer approval. The detective wondered at how a killer such as the woman in front of her had become so subservient so soon, all to a man in a good suit. But was this subservience, or was this another premeditated act? Melanie couldn't work out whether she was giving the woman too much credit or not enough.

'We've actually got footage of you together at Benny's café in the centre of town.' Carter pulled a still shot of Violet sitting opposite Ethan, their smiling expressions clearly visible. 'This is you, isn't it?'

Preston studied the photograph. 'Yes, it looks to be me.'

'And this gentleman here is Ethan Irwill?' Preston nodded by way of responding. 'So, now we've established you do know Ethan Irwill, maybe you can explain to us how it was you met. We're already aware that you accessed his computer remotely to find out about his dark web behaviours, but it's the time before that we're especially interested in. Did someone put you in touch with him somehow?'

Preston looked at Hodder before answering. Melanie saw the lawyer give a subtle shift of his head from one side to the other as though to caution his client, but she looked back to the officers in front of her and said, 'I overheard him and a group of friends talking.' Melanie made a note on the pad in front of her; this explained why none of Ethan's friends had mentioned Violet during the early interviews, and why Kerrick and Gallagher claimed never to have seen the woman before when they'd been re-interviewed. *With that kind of dumb luck working in Preston's favour*, Melanie thought, *the poor blokes never stood a chance.*

'They were talking about who Ethan was screwing, that's how they phrased it, and I remember thinking what a shame it was that such a nice man, nice to look at, was obviously so shallow.'

'Shallow?' Melanie jumped in.

'It was all about sex, not experience. Or that's how it came across.'

'So, why did you pursue him?'

'Curiosity, I think, to see whether I was right.'

'And were you?'

Preston considered this for a second. 'No, no I don't think I was. Ethan wanted the experience to be as real as it possibly could be in the end. He wanted it to be something special, memorable.'

'Not exactly memorable for him.'

'In a way.' Violet sounded thoughtful, nostalgic. 'That was the whole reason for the recording, I suppose. Maybe not the recording itself, but for sharing the recording.'

'Whose idea was that, Violet, yours or Ethan's?' Melanie pushed.

'Ethan's.' She smiled. 'Ethan wanted everyone to see what we'd made; that was part of the deal.' She looked ready to expand but her brief interrupted her.

'You've asked your questions on Ethan Irwill. My client had a contract with the deceased; we'll fight it. What else do you think you have?' Hodder's voice was tight, as though panic was spreading out just beneath the surface. Not that Melanie didn't understand him being unnerved; caught in a trap of evidence, Preston looked like a woman uncorked.

'What exactly will you fight in court, so we're all clear? Contractual murder?' Melanie snapped.

'He wanted it though,' Preston added. 'He was so, so ready.'

'Violet.' Hodder cautioned his client. 'If we're still sticking to this one case then we may as well get the formalities out of the way and get ready for court. Irwill is nothing.'

'I'm sure the jury will be glad to know your thoughts on that,' Melanie spat back.

She felt a ball of something form in the base of her stomach – anger, spite, she couldn't tell. But whatever the feeling was, she suddenly felt as desperate to smite the man in front of her as much as the woman he was representing. She looked at the second folder lying in front of Carter and gave her partner a nudge. He opened the cardboard wallet and retrieved four portraits of four different men positioned on Waller's examination trolleys. He spread the images out in front of Preston and Hodder, and left a deliberate silence before he spoke.

'Could you tell us whether you recognise any of these men?'

'You're alleging that my client killed these individuals too, are you?' Hodder looked from one end of the image line-up to the other. 'You'll have a hard time proving it.'

Melanie ignored the fighting talk. She watched as Preston looked from one man to the next, savouring the images much more than her legal representation had.

'Is there anything you want to tell us about these men, Violet?' Melanie asked, her tone deliberately gentle, as though she might coax information from the woman.

'Detective, I will not let you goad my client–'

'No, and it seems you won't let us conduct a simple interview with her either.' Melanie half-stood and rested her fists on the table. 'We have evidence enough to charge your client with multiple murders; there is no doubt. I'm simply giving her the opportunity to explain her actions, Mr Hodder.'

'That's what you want from her, is it, an outright confession of motive?' Hodder matched Melanie's posture. Detective and lawyer were a shift away from butting heads across the table when Melanie, realising the risks she was taking with such a forceful confrontation, backed down. She dropped into the chair behind her and Hodder sank back too.

'Is that what you'd like, detective, a motive?' Preston asked, her eyes still wandering from one end of the cadaver line-up to the other. Melanie could see something in the woman, a strange kind of fondness that Melanie couldn't marry with the portraits on the table. It was as though she hadn't noticed the crossed aggression between Melanie and Hodder at all. She'd been too engrossed.

'I'd like to understand why this happened, Violet, yes.'

Preston looked up from the evidence spread in front of her. She locked eyes with Melanie and a beat of uncomfortable silence passed between them.

'It will help your case too, if you're shown to be co-operating with the investigation,' Carter added.

'But you're certainly under no obligation,' Hodder said.

Preston held a look with Melanie still. The detective couldn't help but feel as though the other woman was looking for something in her.

'Detective, have you ever wanted something so much that you'd do anything for it?' Preston reached out and rested her fingertips against the corner of Ethan Irwill's photograph. Melanie considered the question; her mind wandered to her first pair of Dr Martens, bought and paid for by a year of working Saturdays and evenings after college. There had been things she wanted, of course; but nothing she wanted this much.

'No, I don't know that I have.' Melanie leaned forward slightly to close the gap between them. 'Is that how you've felt about these men, Violet?'

She shook her head. 'Not all of them, no. Only this one.' She sounded wistful, like a young girl describing her first flush of romance. Preston pulled her hand back from the photograph and said, 'Ethan is the only man I ever really went after.'

'Violet, I cannot stress the dangers of your answers here,' Hodder said, his voice sharp, but Violet continued as though the man hadn't spoken at all.

'When you sleep with someone for the first time, not your

246

first time, but theirs, it's something special, isn't it?' Preston asked. Despite the question, she only made eye contact with the dead men in front of her, as though speaking directly to them. 'When you're someone's first, whether they love you, or come to love you, or whether they feel utter indifference towards you, they carry you with them. You'll always be the person they gave that experience to.'

'Is this a sexual thing for you, Violet?'

She almost laughed. 'No, detective, not in the least. But it's the same idea, see. I'll always be the person they gave their lives to.'

'But they're gone now. They can't carry the experience with them,' Melanie said, her tone gentle again. She felt as though she were getting somewhere and nowhere all at once.

Preston pulled her eyes together in a flash of confusion. 'It must be the other way around then. I carry them with me. They'll never share this with someone else and that's so, well, so special. Don't you think?' She looked directly at Melanie. 'They were all ready to die, detective, they had their reasons aplenty. But they also knew they'd never do it for themselves.'

'So, you were helping them?' Carter asked, his tone flat. Melanie nudged him underneath the table.

'We were helping each other. They wanted to die, and I wanted to kill them. It was a two-way arrangement and it led to the collection that you've probably found by now.'

'A collection.' Melanie latched on to the word. 'Is that how you see it?'

'Some women want shoes, some women want dolls, some–'

'Okay, it's time to cut this nonsense,' Hodder interrupted, addressing the room at large rather than one specific individual. 'My client has given you what you asked for.'

'Has she though?' Carter said, frustration barely concealed in his tone.

'I think she's just about to start giving us what we asked for,' Melanie added.

'Unless you have hard proof then you're working with completely circumstantial evidence and a half-confession that won't be worth a damn when we bring in a temporary insanity defence,' Hodder replied, his tone spiteful. 'I don't think there's any worry for us on what a courtroom will make of this sh–'

'It's not circumstantial evidence, though,' Preston cut across the man. 'And I'm not sure you're qualified to assess any levels of insanity, Mr Hodder.' She looked over her shoulder to give her lawyer a hard glare before she turned back to Melanie. Preston looked with the same searching expression as before, but there was something sad about it now. 'The officers actually have everything they need.'

Melanie stood in front of the evidence board, her hands buried in her pockets and her head tipped back, to get a good look at everything that had been pinned together over the last two days. There was still one body unaccounted for – despite the search team having overturned the garden of the house the man owned – and that would be something to bring up with Violet at a later date. But for now they needed to wait. Melanie replayed Archer's advice – 'Wait until he asks for a deal.' She took a deep inhale to try to steady her nerves. She'd never waited out a case like this before, and it was setting her on edge.

'The woman's a bloody psycho. I don't know why we aren't back in there with the footage, boss,' Carter said, waving around the still image of Violet that had been pulled from the snuff film. 'We can pin her to the wall with this, and then this is all over.'

'Do you think she's a psycho, Carter?' Melanie asked. 'Is it that simple?'

'She wants to collect dead men. What else does that make her?'

Melanie didn't like his tone. 'She wants to help them die.'

'Which makes her a cliché at best. She's an angel of death. Isn't she?'

'She's hardly a caregiver, though. Isn't that the point of an angel of death?'

'Maybe she thinks she is a caregiver,' Burton added.

'Who knows what the woman thinks. We should be back in there with her, boss.'

'Do you have a plan? Is that what this is?'

Melanie snorted. 'We always have a plan, Burton, sometimes the plan is just waiting.' She turned around to survey the office, which was still packed with members of her own team and others who were working to manage the onslaught of evidence that was falling into their laps. Carter was right; she had enough to pin Preston to the wall, but Melanie was determined not to reveal more evidence to Hodder than she needed to – and that meant waiting. 'Let me know if there are any developments, would you?' she said, before pacing into her office. She closed the door behind her, dropped down into her seat and picked up the handset of her desk phone. Melanie was midway through dialling Archer's extension when a knock came at the door. She sighed. 'A development already.' She dropped the phone back into its rest. 'Come in.'

Burton pushed the door open and took a stride into the room. 'Hodder's here.'

The two shared a knowing look. Melanie followed Burton out of the office and into the communal space where there were witnesses to whatever conversation was about to unfold. Before Burton retreated to her own desk Melanie caught her arm.

'Cover the evidence board.' Melanie closed the distance between herself and Hodder. The lawyer was having a good look around the room and Melanie hoped that Burton had got to the board before the man had seen anything worthwhile. 'If you want another interview you'll have to give myself and DS Carter more notice than this I'm afraid.'

His mouth curled slightly at one side. Melanie was ready for a growl to emerge. 'You know full well this isn't about another interview.'

'No? What can we help you with then? We're a little busy up here.' She gestured to the room around her.

'So I see. You've obviously got quite a lot of material to work with here, so I'll make this easier for you and your team, detective. I'd like to cut a deal for my client.'

Melanie bit back on the beginnings of a laugh. 'I'm sorry, how are you making things easier then?'

'You can halt the investigations now. She'll plead guilty for the murder of Ethan Irwill and admit fraud for the properties that she gained from the others. It'll be a life sentence and justice will be served.'

'I thought you wanted to go for a temporary insanity defence.'

Hodder sighed. 'Miss Preston has no interest in an insanity plea, which sort of proves my point.' He held his hands palm up in a show of defeat. 'I've warned her of the risks in going to court and leaving herself open to additional charges. I was hoping you would be good-natured enough to take our deal and leave the other cases be, if we're being frank, detective.'

Melanie frowned. It sounded like a strange version of justice. 'Tempting as the offer is–'

'Now, come on, this case has been a grind. Aren't you ready to be done with it all?'

'So, Violet agrees to this deal, does she?'

'Of course. She knows a good opportunity when she sees one.'

'And it is an extremely good opportunity,' Melanie agreed. 'For you.'

'You'd benefit from this deal as well, DI Watton, don't think otherwise. We both get rid of a case that we'd rather not be working on.'

Melanie looked around the office. Despite the interruption that Hodder had caused, every member of the team had buckled down to their work again. She thought of the hours they'd worked, the evidence they'd found – the ironclad case they'd built. 'It's kind of you to make this sort of an offer, Mr Hodder.' She closed the gap between them so her next comment was audible only to the lawyer. 'But I'll be giving the CPS enough to nail your client to the fucking wall before this is over.'

44

Court appearances had always made Melanie feel uncomfortable, even though she'd been on the right side of the law from day one. She'd spent the morning sitting in on Violet's trial, waiting to be called for evidence. But the proceedings had been suspended for the afternoon without even a mention of Melanie's evidence and the officer – along with the other potential witnesses – had been excused back to her normal duties for the remainder of the day. She balanced her mobile phone between her ear and her shoulder as she scanned herself through the station's security system, dropping her card into her breast pocket when she was finished.

'No, no, I think that's a really good idea,' she said, treading her way through the winding corridors back toward the sanctuary of the MIT office. She was one floor off when Burton caught up with her, the officer trailing her superior by a step or two. 'Okay, that sounds really good to me. I'm back in the office now, but maybe we can pick this up later. ... Brilliant. I'll be leaving at around six. ... Well, Government work isn't quite in the same league as academia. ... I know, I know. We'll talk later.'

She extinguished the phone call as she arrived outside the office door.

'Are we pulling someone in from behind the piles of books?' Burton asked, following her boss into the communal space.

'I'm sorry?' Melanie looked around the room as she spoke. Although there was still evidence box on top of evidence box, the office looked a little closer to normal than it had done for some weeks now, and Melanie was relieved at the makeover.

'The phone call. Academia.'

Melanie felt her face flush, but she tried to ignore it. 'It was Hilda Addair.'

'Ah, expert witness?' Burton already looked near to distraction with something she'd found on her desk.

'No, actually. It was a personal call.'

The junior officer's head snapped up and her eyes searched for her boss' across the room. 'Oh.' She smiled. 'Oh, I see.'

'What do you see?' Carter wandered out from Melanie's office. 'I've finished signing off on the housing reports that Fairer and Read put together if you want to look over them before they're filed. On your desk.'

'Cheers, Carter.' Melanie walked between the officers to head for her open doorway.

'What do you see?'

'The boss was on a personal call,' Burton said, her voice bursting with what Melanie thought was excitement. 'With Hilda Addair.'

'Oh.'

Melanie turned to face Carter.

'Oh, I see.' His face cracked into a smile. 'Christ, good for you. It's about time.'

Melanie cocked an eyebrow at him. 'That's not an appropriate comment for the workplace, Carter.' She turned back toward her doorway and walked into her empty office.

'What about outside of the workplace over a curry and a pint?'

'Maybe,' she shouted back, and she heard her colleagues erupt in teenaged giggling.

Melanie looked over the small mounds of paperwork that had appeared on her desk over the morning. With more evidence there came more files to be opened, approved and eventually closed, and the Preston case appeared never-ending with evidence. They'd got as far as the trial without finding the final body in the case – Neil Quinton, the only one who had someone for a while – but Melanie couldn't shake her concerns over it. She skimmed the row of Post-it notes that were lined up behind her phone, in the hope that there would be a message from one search team or another. They'd found more properties attached to Violet and her many monikers, but wherever they searched turned up empty.

'Still nothing on that last one?' Morris said as she appeared in the doorway.

'Neil.' Melanie sighed. She'd even tried to track down the colleague who'd reported Quinton missing but he'd changed his number, stopped calling, maybe moved on. 'There doesn't seem to be any leads, no. Any more properties to report?'

'Nothing that's on her laptop, her online storage, or in her emails.'

'I'm not just leaving a body out there.' She rested her forehead against her balled up hand. 'Christ, the thought of it is ridiculous. She won't give it up though, Morris. Wherever that man is, she won't tell a bloody soul.'

'You don't think she'll crack in court?'

Melanie shook her head. 'She's kept up her silence for this long. I doubt it'll change.'

'You've done everything you can, though. You can't look forever.' She took a further step into the office and set a folder down on Melanie's guest chair. 'They're all of my case notes from Preston, start to finish, minus the bit about Fairer and I setting up a fake online profile to try to catch a killer without our superior's permission.' The junior officer closed one eye and screwed her face into an expression that suggested she was ready for a reprimand. But nothing came.

'You're lucky I'm in a good mood,' Melanie said, her tone playful. 'I'll leave it out of my report if you'll keep it out of yours. Make sure that Fairer knows the same, alright?'

The team spent the rest of the day batting questions back and forth to ready themselves for giving evidence. Melanie fenced questions too, and signed off on final reports until her own signature looked like that of a stranger. She rubbed at her eyes and then closed them entirely as she slumped down into her desk chair, giving herself permission to breathe and reboot for a moment.

'Exhausted?'

When Melanie looked up, Archer was blocking her doorway. The DI leapt to her feet and tried to find the energy for professionalism.

'Mel, please. Sit down.' Archer came the rest of the way into the room and pushed the door closed behind her. She cleared away a pile of paperwork from the visitor's chair and made herself comfortable, with the documents she'd moved now resting on her lap. 'Is this Morris' work?' she asked, looking down at the folder.

'It is. She's looked high and low for another property, but she's had to admit defeat.' Melanie heard the defeat in her own voice too.

'That's actually what I'm here about.'

'You've found somewhere?'

'No. I'm afraid if Morris can't find somewhere then we're stumped because I certainly don't have any leads myself. That said, I had a phone call from the prison this afternoon.'

'Hodder?'

'Violet.'

Melanie's head snapped up at the announcement. 'She's talking?'

'In exchange for something.'

Melanie busied herself with papers. 'So, she wants to cut her own deal.'

'Five years off whatever her sentence is, which isn't much, considering she'll get repeated life sentences for the murders she's being tried for.' Archer made the request sound reasonable, but Melanie wasn't as convinced.

'Then why cut a deal at all?'

'Power? To get one over on Hodder? Us? Does it matter?'

Melanie thought for a moment, but she really wasn't sure of the answer. 'You told me not to cut a deal. Does that go out the window when we're dealing directly with the criminals rather than their briefs?'

Archer sighed. 'No, it goes out the window when it's something you actually want.' She stood from her seat. 'You need to know when to back down on things, Mel, and this might just be one of those occasions. You're a good police officer, you know that much, so don't go letting stubbornness get in the way of a clean sweep on a case.' She turned to leave, her hand outstretched for the door handle.

'A clean sweep?'

Archer turned to face her junior. 'A clean sweep. She'll give us Neil Quinton's location, if we barter with the judge for a reduced sentence.'

So, it was a power play, Melanie thought. One final act of dominance before the killer lost the ability to barter with anything other than prison currency. The thought of giving in to the demands of a murderer made Melanie feel uncomfortable in her own skin, but she couldn't shake the thought that Archer was right. In the grand scheme of things, could bowing down be the right thing to do?

'Do you honestly need to think about this, Mel?'

'No,' Melanie answered, her tone firm. 'No, tell her we'll cut a deal for a clean sweep. Wherever her last victim is, we're going to bring him home.'

The End